CHOCOLATE DUNGEON

JUSTIN ROGERS

authorHOUSE®

AuthorHouse™
1663 Liberty Drive
Bloomington, IN 47403
www.authorhouse.com
Phone: 833-262-8899

Published by AuthorHouse 07/29/2020

ISBN: 978-1-7283-6359-2 (sc)
ISBN: 978-1-7283-6358-5 (e)

Print information available on the last page.

This book is printed on acid-free paper.

1

So many older people say "If I knew then what I know now?"

That's how I wish I could have started that week in 1980 before I left for the army, a morning I woke to yet another 24 hours of depression, as far as I was concerned — having to again get out of bed for work at the Grand Avenue Grocery next door, facing the same people and things again and again until I wanted to scream.

I was so insecure, so nervous, almost afraid I might trip over my own shadow. But I couldn't – it couldn't – be ignored that I was almost nineteen.

I looked in the mirror and it was as if it could steal my soul, claw out my eyes courtesy of a Bloody Mary chant done in the dark. On that morning, I probably would have liked seeing some un-earthly soul in the mirror other than myself.

I walked to my window, with the peeling green paint of the back wall of the grocery – my dream job – facing me. Maybe that building would play a part in finding who I was?

Shower time. Walking out of my bedroom, I look back at it for one of the last times before Saturday's departure. Car parts all over, my room the auto junkyard, soon for grocery storage.

They never got assembled, but perhaps that was good, for because of it I had had many cherished times with Buck, my boss at the grocery, sitting in our yard putting it together, talking, I trying to feel like, well, so what if he wanted something? Who's perfect?, deep down not accepting that I was just being used.

The clock. 50 minutes until work. Can't dare be late. Means that much.

Hooray, no school. A year and two months since high school. The ceremony that was as American as apple pie.

I had never really seen anywhere but Fell – a small Missouri town that got its name from a meteor that crashed into it – and nearby St. Louis. Those two together seemed huge, even though they weren't, just familiar. Like anyone else, I did what I could, where I could: working at the grocery, trying to be a good son.

I had the obsessiveness that ran in our family, "racing thoughts," if that's what you wanted to call Obsessive-Compulsive Disorder - though having overcome some of it with medication - I having long ago learned to deal with my mother talking about the same things again and again. She didn't believe in meds.

But even with medication, as you will see, I obsess a lot - still it not meaning I'm not smart - ever trapped in my essential dungeon of chocolate until I get better by finding myself (I obsess a lot about essentials). Ever the question: Who am I? Sometimes in my life there is a dead silence and I feel all alone, deep in thought for a moment. And you will hear me mention feeling like being on an island, if not a deserted one at times, also deep in thought.

You will see that I constantly compare my life to the lottery and the prom I went to and the constant war with myself because I am a perfectionist. And again and again my life fills with this dead silence.

I tried, gave a part of myself to mother. It did sometimes seem for nothing, for never any change. Mom's life was peanut butter.

I reached the zero percent thrill of the bathroom. I would later be captive there, not knowing it then. It was like any other part of the house: tiles that spoke to me with their age, bits of toothpaste on the sink where I had been messy.

Mom and I were anything but neat, my room always a mess, mom leaving empty peanut butter jars scattered around the living room.

I do so love mom, hating to see her fall into Buck's trap. But she would and for it I would have to prepare mentally; accept it or go crazy.

The bathroom was going to be a shrine to my memory. I had been in it so many times. There were almost too many memories to leave. Still, I needed to. I knew it was more of a risk not going in the army. I had to try the thing; take the chance. And I would. But it was scary to leave.

My toothbrush sat on the sink on one that had Bugs Bunny on it, leftover from when, of course, I was a kid, the Bugs one almost seeming like an angel trying to tell me something; telling me to hang in there and that my childhood had been happier than I might think.

I looked in the mirror again, smiling at who I saw. Maybe things weren't so bad.

I could smell the pancakes, it blending strangely with the smell of the peanut butter.

I cursed. Was I the only one that had problems? It seemed that way. But everyone had something to deal with, I just had a face readable: young appearance, bulging red eyes.

Racing to the steps, I sat. I would miss them. So many memories embedded: my parents walking down them in matrimony to the grocery aisles saying "I Do." The town watching. Steps a comfortable place to sit and think. First about what school would be like, and now I pondered the army.

The steps had not changed. I had. And the sameness of imagining Darlene and I walking down those steps together in matrimony too. An impossible probability, but I hung on.

I didn't want to get up from the steps. I wished I could sit on them forever instead of face the world.

But I wasn't growing in that house. I needed to experience things.

Change in a few days? Some. Virginia. The army base. But taking me with me.

Only go forward. And today's all I've got.

As I sat there, it was as if each step was like an alien trying to tell me something. All my life and my mother much of her life had known these steps. Ever would I think of them, almost hating that I was so sentimental. But the steps were very soon to be forever a memory. They would have crates of soup cans banging upward against them instead of my tennis shoes. And I didn't want that. I hated changes; held on to what was.

The steps held such significance for me because they almost were me. After all, I had to learn to climb them. Like all kids, I at least went down them stomach first. Then, of course, like learning to swim, I ran down them the regular way. And I watched our dogs grow old and lose the energy to climb them.

I knew how many steps there were: 13. I remembered counting them so long ago, as soon as I knew how to count. And now I would be a number, leaving the steps to fight those across the world who grew up on steps thinking too. They, too, having left their mothers and home-cooked meals for the universal iron discipline of the military, which all but nurtures, but supposedly protects my country's people. Hopefully leading to agreement - what keeps the world going at all - the only thing that ever has, just as much as only a small group of people has ever changed it.

I'm sitting on – and surrounded by – what was my childhood. Never had I lived anywhere else. But what if I had? What if I had lived in 12 houses? Would it have mattered? I still would have been me. Taking myself to house after house, steps or no steps, I would have remembered them all as significant as I had this one: this place of mine to give way to soup.

I accepted that that was how it was going to be. Such was as real as not wanting to get out of bed in the morning, not wanting to get up for school for 12 years, and the same for work. Just as much as I had to fight myself not to be lazy, I was going to have to give Buck Mellon his way in terms of real estate. I was, essentially, forever his slave. Partly because of circumstances, and partly to have someone to talk to. Extra grocery storage was Buck's dream and I knew, like Russia wanting to have all the land in the world, Buck would always want a little more storage. Human nature yes, it was, to not be satisfied.

Pathetic, yes. Sad and pathetic, and it did no good to cry, be it from change, be it from unfairness. As a soldier in war, anyway, I would find out about unfairness from what I would see and go through.

And yet within me indeed was a truer war. How could I help the world if I couldn't win a war with myself? I had yet to know just who that was in that mirror and on those steps.

Maybe someday, after fighting against fellow, war-ravaged countries that unfortunately was what had and always would make up the history of the world, I might find a way to give a part of myself to some faraway soldier seemingly an emotional mirror image of me, he never stopping his dreams and hopes either.

2

I looked at the front door. It's significance, part of my comings and goings from there: walking out of it to play in the back storeroom of the the grocery which no one ever knew about; to go with my mother as a small child to peanut butter eating conventions in St. Louis; to work at my dream job.

Into the kitchen, to eat. Food itself the very stuff that had weaved webs of soap-opera-like living for me and the few others in my life on that lonely road. I munched on bacon, thinking about the dead pigs that had had their lives taken so I could enjoy my meal. Still, to have a meal was part of why God gave us animals. But still not right to take a life, no matter the reason. And so animals –namely those killed for food - also had to experience life being unfair. I wasn't the only one with problems.

Eating a hearty breakfast, I wonder why mom only eats peanut butter. Why addicted?

I feel comfortable as my mother stands behind me, washing dishes.

"Thanks mom for breakfast" I said, remembering saying that at five years old.

"You're welcome, dear" she said lovingly.

We loved each other, but needed to be away from each other.

"I know I've probably sheltered you too much, James. I'm sorry."

"Mom, you're wonderful" I responded.

I tried to hide feelings of wishing mom wasn't a sucker. She was about to be swindled, and by someone who had long swindled everyone else in town, and she hadn't a clue as to it. It was getting toward my last chances to warn her about it. Indeed, I wondered, would I not be doing my part as a family member to protect another relative, another loved one from harm, whether direct or indirect? But I just ate, feeling powerless.

The kitchen filled with a dead silence, as if there was nothing to do or talk about, like the summer boredom that came while waiting for school to start.

Would it be more lively in the house with siblings? I would, of course, not ever know. But I had never known any other way but being mom's one and only, either.

The lazy part of me caused me to keep sitting there instead of getting over to work to punch in. I loved my work, even though I was abused: by Buck, and by – it seemed – everyone else. I had been abused by so many people over so long that I, at some point, had quit trying to have friends.

In an ideal world, I would have a say in what happened: in the grocery; in the town. Both, I admitted to myself, I wanted to control as much as Buck did, which I knew wasn't right; I should not feel wanting to take Buck's place of being town dictator in the way of owning and thus controlling the towns almost only economic force: the grocery. But the truth was I had always wanted just that, and for that reason, I would come back here, re-apply to the grocery and pray for rehire, even if I worked under Jamie. The grocery and its cashier – Darlene Staley – were my life.

I was almost ready to leave, again bracing for the pressures of the day. It took bravery.

I look at mom. She staring out the kitchen window and dreaming as much as me. She wished for my father – who had died in war (though we lived comfortably from life insurance) – to be alive. But worse for her, I knew, was that she did not see the wedding of her and Buck coming: a seemingly shotgun wedding of force.

But wish this, wish that. The seeds were sown. I couldn't tell Buck off. For the sake of a dream job. For the sake of the love I worked with.

It was almost here. Final confrontation. It would have mom caught between disownment and missing me. Loved mom. Like me, she just had too many problems to help someone else.

Her addiction to peanut butter – now Buck knowing because he riled it out of me years ago as we worked on car parts together – could be her doom in a double way: harming her health as well as leading to a fated wedding ring on her finger. In businesses name. And nothing more. Purely and simply, it was all just a profit-making machine. Were both me and mom destined to die alive? Die on the inside?

And so my mother was looking out the kitchen window to a world with no windows. To nice people in the world finishing last. And mom and I were too nice. Too kind indeed.

How could I help my mother so she wouldn't have to go through this? How could I be a hero, a renaissance man, the wizard of all wizards of eighteen-year-old men?

If only I could do magic. Weave my web of character and honesty that was also noticed, instead of watch conniving deceit too manipulative for my gullible mother to realize? No magic wands in this world, and probably not in others, if they did exist. And so if there were other planets to live on, I would not be any happier, as they were probably just reflections of earth, whatever planet you lived on being the same. Problems there too, and likely the same ones.

I finished my last piece of bacon, tasting what again fueled the whole sick cycle of my situation: food. In the weirdest possible way, it was the tool. Getting to people's stomachs got them to agree. Through taste. Through smell. The senses were such suckers. Too useful for their own good, as much as my causing people to have to think worked against me because maybe I was too smart for my own good. If psychic was the sixth sense, maybe what I went through with people was the seventh: Far too intellectual and eccentric for my town. As if Buck kept me trapped in a mirror ignorant, and I watched mirrors of myself flying toward windows to worlds with answers, but just missing going into them, unlike that brilliant light you are supposed to see and go into forever when you die, and all your questions are answered. Oh again and again, that question of what was death? What was living? At any given time, which one was I essentially in? I thought about it so much it was dizzying.

I especially thought about death, as it seemed like it would be more comforting than being alive. When you lived, at least for me, you had to deal with things that may never be resolved. With death, it may just be peace. Serenity. What's never fixed not mattering anymore. How awful – uncomforting – it would be on Judgement Day when the dead became living again, back to their old problems? Surely God wouldn't do that to them any more than he wouldn't let things be better for me after my life – almost all of it to be spent in this little Missouri hammock – was expended?

Was the problem that I needed to find out if and how I had lived before, with that hypnotism they called past-life regression? Even so, maybe it was that I had never lived it up at all in this life? No one outside this house had ever really opened up to me. Instead, they just wanted me to make them laugh, or give them a ride somewhere; I gave a part of myself to some degree but really it was just other people taking, grabbing from me whatever they could.

I had worked at friendships: kids living across the meteor "hole" who used to like me but, somehow, over the years, I turned them off with my "personality," and we grew apart while living so close to each other in the same little town. That kind of thing. And so it was more than Meteor Canyon – as we called the huge gash that divided the town - that divided us. It was me. A gaping canyon within me of no confidence.

3

It was indeed interesting how I had always lived in that town whose only interesting feature had always been Meteor Canyon. It was a huge hole in the ground that went very deep, in fact rivaling the Grand Canyon, also believed to have been formed by a meteor crashing into it. But Meteor Canyon, to me, also came to be what I blamed my problems – my boredom – on.

Yes, St. Louis was close by. But I wanted to see more than that. I wanted to be where the meteor had come from. Far away on some planet no one knew about. But instead, I seemed to be on the most boring street in America, which led to the most exciting place I knew: St. Louis with its famous arch.

An arch and a meteor canyon. Wow. Surely there was more to the world than that. But perhaps I needed to find the world - inside me - that was who I was instead.

I again wished I could stay like when I had just been sitting on the steps - be seated there at the breakfast table forever. How nice that would be, to never get up. Never go out in the world and face life's problems. Just sit there eating bacon forever. That was heaven: eternally doing something you enjoyed. And so hell had to be forever doing something you didn't like, such as putting up with Buck.

But I knew I needed to be fair with Buck, even in private thoughts that no one else knew about. After all, people could sense what you thought about them, and Buck was smart and, in an instant, could end my job forever.

That made me shudder. Then everything would be down the drain. I needed the grocery for a reference. And I might – well I did – want to come back after the war and work at the grocery for the rest of my life. This grocery had been my life, as always I had grown up next to it and waited to be old enough to work there. It was Buck's life and significant to mom because she got married in it. And it was the social center of that town half related to me. A town with nothing in it but a grocery. Sad, all the people here who would never branch out to see more than that, simply because of the old, ancient fear of the unknown, something common to all people.

It was getting down to the last minute. I was so glad for my job. There was nothing to do at home, and I didn't have any school work to do as I had chosen not to go to college. I had never liked school. All one did, as far as I saw it, was sit in a desk. And yet I wondered if maybe, just maybe, I should plan on going to the reunions. Because even though there were people I did not want to see, there were also people I did want to see, people that had shaped me.

Indeed, I had known many of them since kindergarten. And I would board the bus with some of them on Saturday. And off we, the boys from Fell, would go to war together.

How, though, did one define war? Was it more than just not getting along? Wasn't it more not understanding oneself, and how that caused a lack of finding a solution to things? Were soldiers just confused individuals being ordered by the confused? Maybe I could be the one soldier who could lead everyone else out of confusion and out of the war with my insight? Maybe I could be the one to make that difference? Maybe I could show that, perhaps, fighting with guns was not even necessary, because maybe all that needed to be done was talk things out, and maybe have countries trade a thing or two to make everyone feel better? But perhaps even more, be at peace with oneself – aside from with another country – in the first place?

During that last week at the grocery, I remembered something I once read:

"There is always enough money for war, but never enough for education."

How true.

For indeed knowledge –talking things out – was the power that could stop the needless killing of wars that no one ever really won. And just as well, my war with myself and with educating the people in that town to see beyond my young face which I hated was worth more – worth winning people over as to - than all the chocolate that had ever been in the grocery basement storeroom. It kept adding up to the same thing: winning a personal war was more worthwhile than an actual war on a battlefield.

Because how could one win the world if one first did not win with oneself on one's inside?

And so there were two wars going on in "my" world: Wars on the outside of people, and very real, personal wars on the inside of each of us which, even though most people looked confident, were being fought every second of every day because most people were scared inside, I just couldn't cover it up as they could. I stood out in my fears. I was a dead giveaway completely when it came to the emotions showing on my face. In short, I was predictable. People knew what I was thinking. And they knew I was not happy. Would the army be any better?

4

Back and forth I went between standing there bagging groceries and seeing Buck's eyes trying to turn everyone against me, it only ever seeming to happen to me. Patriotic music blared from the grocery speakers to make every day like the Fourth of July, part of Buck's plan to brainwash me into wanting to leave for soldierhood. It was so loud I had sometimes been able to hear it at home. Amazing he would go to so much trouble to manipulate one person, or better said two, as Buck had long been working on my mother who, whenever she came in to shop, Buck would say to her "he would make a fine soldier." And that was how it had been as long as I could remember, even when I came in with my mother at five years old to shop. It had been going on that long and too long and everything defining the long, dead energy of a sicko.

Flags hung everywhere, too, combining in an un-patriotic way of blending with the smell of the fine european chocolate that seeped up from down the stairs. Such smell had been happening ever since that day, again, Buck and I worked on the car parts together in my yard, me naïve or gullible or whatever you want to call it, but Buck managed to get the conversation to be about my mother and found out about the peanut butter.

My mother would hide all the jars lying around when company came over (it was always only relatives, and even they hardly ever came over), and so when Buck came to my birthday parties, he did not know – at least, again, before I told him about her addiction to it – as my mother used air freshener to get rid of the smell. I would always regret that I had often foolishly believed – if only because I wanted to - that I could be proud to call Buck Walter Mellon, Jr. friend.

And Buck Mellon came to know about my mother's love for a peanut butter eating *contest*. What an important piece of the puzzle of a ticking time bomb I couldn't put together because I didn't know exactly what he was going to pull, just that it would have to do with food. At least I was guessing.

I watched tourist after tourist pour in the door, the sad saga of my situation continuing. When you bagged groceries, you couldn't stop. You always had to be doing something while you were on the clock: bagging, gathering carts outside, sweeping. But it was not only the job I had waited all my life for but the only job around at all, at least that I could do. Only the high school and a funeral home – aside from the grocery - were on this side of town – this side of the meteor gap – where mom and I lived. And I knew neither teaching nor funeral work was for me. Indeed both were among the hardest professions there were. Just my luck they were all I lived by besides the grocery, alias other job prospects.

As I watched the tourists scurrying all over I wished it could be me on vacation, with nothing better to do than going to see an arch over a waterfront in St. Louis that was, to me, really nothing. Still, to them it would be fresh. Something they usually told me that they had never seen before. And they would talk about the ride on it they had heard about, such being a bumpy elevator ride for nine dollars, the price of which had gone up steadily – like with anything else – over the years.

From seemingly the world over they stopped off at Fell, and from there rented cars would fill the grocery parking lot; no one able to find their car because they all looked alike. But I was getting paid, I would tell them, so I didn't mind helping them find their vehicles.

Not that there weren't times when I did, in fact, honestly feel like throwing in the towel, that is, walk out. Quit. Go home to mother — the whole bit. But I couldn't. I had waited too long for what I had and for what I hoped: future ownership and management of the grocery, which my boss wanted anything but to give me.

As it went with men, I was my career and lived to make the grocery the best it could be just as much as Buck. As much as we fought, and as much as we wanted a piece of what each other had, we had a special male bond that I knew could never be the same somewhere else again in my life, because you never had relationships like the ones you had had since birth.

Thus it went on: Buck wanted my mother's will, and I wanted "his" grocery. And since I was old enough to remember, that had defined both our lives, Buck being afraid when I was born, I knew, because – being a boy – I would be more economically valuable and so all the more he would want to get rid of me, jealous that I could somehow rise above him in business. Get me out of the way so he could marry my mother for that house. And such took manipulation, of which I was in the way.

And what about when I was out of the way? What would it be like when I came home to visit, and Buck was my stepfather? I had always known that was coming, too, and it would be hard. Buck – despite how well he knew me – would never replace the father I never knew.

As I was outside gathering carts, I looked up at my bedroom window, to the room soon to be filled with soup cans — something I had no control over. I felt like a weakling when it came to the whole situation, and I was almost glad for the summer sun to be shining in my eyes, feeling maybe it would be better to be blinded by it.

5

Jamie came in, twirling his tennis racket. I wondered how Jamie got money, as from what I knew, he had never had a job. But Jamie's personality had something mine did not: to cause people to, well, not give him a hard time. Jamie could get away with being lazy and with, it seemed, everything else people didn't like me for, such as not having a girlfriend. It looked like Jamie had no friends, but he was master at faking a confident look. His brain developed.

The grocery was destined to go to Jamie, which crushed me. How could Buck leave it to him? Jamie had no experience in running anything. He just knew about playing tennis and getting money from his parents. But no one ever said life was fair, and if the best I would get was coming back from the army and working under Jamie at the grocery, then I would have to accept it. I scrubbed floors spotless for Buck, and I would keep loving the grocery – my dream and second home – enough that I would scrub floors for Jamie too one day.

As I bagged, Jamie looked at me smiling, a mean smile that couldn't be anything but one hundred percent stuck up. I wanted to tell him off so bad. And yet I was looking at my future boss, and so I couldn't say a word.

Then he went into Buck's office, and he and Buck closed the door and I could hear them laughing. I knew when I was being made fun of. It was so sad. I did so much for the grocery and got no appreciation for it, just a measly paycheck.

I looked at Darlene as she did the register. Her splendid figure and long blonde hair. Beautiful. Impossible for men not to fall in love with her. Though in truth she was insecure, a fact I did not yet know.

"Ready for the army?" said Darlene. Then she winked. That got me excited that she might be in love with me. I entertained the thought, as joyful as when it was time for my break. But to no avail was it. She just saw that kid that bagged groceries. And I hated that.

Then things started happening all at once. There was a line of customers. And a spill in the back. And carts outside to be rounded up. And I was the only one to do any of it. And somehow, just like getting to work right on time every day, I got them all done. And yet again, I asked myself why? For I was likely to have none of the grocery someday.

Yes, it was a good feeling to work. No one liked work or school. But I knew if I weren't productive, I would go crazy. I had to have my work. I would lose my mind sitting home all day watching TV, not to mention I also wouldn't have money for anything.

And so there I stood, wishing I could trade places with the many people around me – fellow employees; tourist after tourist that I served; Jamie. And yet, I could only be me. I could only be on my little island playing the role I had played since the day I was born: myself.

6

Blasted Buck, yet I hardly had anyone else to talk to, deep down hating him as I stood there bagging, he manipulating, using me to get to Ann, and always had. I knew why, though deep down, like going through a tragic death, I tried to deny it.

But the fact was there – Buck had just hired me due to always knowing my mother. And to find out more about her, purely to move closer to wooing her with what went right along with peanut butter. And so Buck always had the grocery full of chocolate.

No matter how anyone felt, it would always come out the same in the end: Buck not caring about anyone but himself. That by then obvious. But still for years I had not realized it, clinging to the glimmer of hope that Buck could be a friend and not just a boss or acquaintance.

If I just knew what he was going to do. Then maybe I could change its course. But Buck was clever. He had

planned it out for too long for anyone but Buck himself –
and maybe his henchman Jamie – to know what was going
to take place at that lonely house next door where I had lived
for almost 19 years and was soon to leave for two homes:
the grocery basement storeroom - in which Buck even had a
bathroom and a shower for whoever was grocery porter - and
then an army barracks.

Darlene smiled at me. A sign of hope she was in love
with me? I spoke to Darlene in a low tone because I did not
want Buck to hear what I was saying:

"I am glad I'm out of here, Darlene. I'm tired of breaking
my back for really nothing."

Darlene looked at me with pity. I hated it when people
felt sorry for me. Why did I have to give an impression that
made people feel that way about me? Was I that bad off?

"I don't blame you, James. If I were you at your young,
budding age, I would want to move on too."

Jealous of the conversation between Darlene and I, Buck
came over and said to me "my son" which was a way of
saying I looked young. Oh, time and time again I had to
prove myself; prove my manhood. Oh, how glad indeed I
was that I was almost out of there.

Darlene said:

"We need to have some goodbye party for James. He's
a hard worker and I, for one, will miss his dependability".

Buck showed no interest, but remembering his stake with Ann suddenly, quickly said:

"Oh yes, yes, James deserves everything we can give him."

That I didn't buy.

"James is like a teacher," Darlene said thoughtfully,

"he never receives the recognition he deserves for his effort."

While I appreciated the compliment, I knew it would not change Buck's business-minded selfishness.

"Very true. Very true," Buck said in a tone that sounded like he did not mean it,

"I reckon military bases all over the world could use James's abilities. And so the USA is lucky to have him."

Such comments just made me hate Buck all the more instead of being flattered. It was all a show. Buck was an actor, and the people who were close to him were puppets.

"I agree" said Darlene with a big Miss America like smile, agreeing with Buck like everyone did because he could manipulate people with his eyes and because she needed a job.

Patriotic music blasted from the speakers as the three of us stood there, but I hardly felt any patriotism. To me, both Buck and Darlene had said enough. I didn't want any more "convenient" compliments. It just made me all the more tired of a situation that was so sad and had been going on for much too long.

"I am proud to serve my country" I said, bowing, not sure how much I meant it as well as not sure who I was.

The tourist customers all clapped, and Buck and Darlene patted me on the back.

"We're proud of you" said Buck.

I knew though that Buck's good moods were temporary, and he would yell at me for something soon.

"You can do anything" said Darlene during the applause.

I wished more than anything that, if I could really "do anything", I could win Darlene's heart in love and marriage – my other dream besides owning the grocery – something I knew deep down also wasn't going to happen.

Then the "party," so to speak, ended, the tourist customers cleared, and Buck was back to being holed up in his office again. Nothing was going to change. But I had long known that.

Being realistic kept me from being disappointed by the permanent non-change of the situation. As I bagged I looked at the door of Buck's office, closed, almost wanting to knock it down and physically strangle Buck just enough to scare him, partially feeling that it wouldn't matter if I did or not because my mother was going to cut me out of the will either way anyway.

7

Finally, I was off work. The woods stood in front of me and, like the sea, could be very dangerous. There could be drug dealers hiding, not wanting me in the woods. One could get lost.

But for me, there had never been any reason except one to go into the deep Missouri wilderness: Dale. He had been a vagrant, with always the same tent site as long as I could remember. He had been someone to talk to – a man in my life to learn from – when Buck wasn't in a good mood to chat.

And, too, there was the food. I snuck food to Dale almost every day to have someone to talk to about things. I couldn't bring any from home, or my mother would know something was up. She certainly wouldn't like it. I could hear her saying "We can't support the whole world. We can hardly support ourselves."

And so it was, then, that I used my grocery discount to feed almost my only friend who never took a shower, just swam in the river every few days, having no other way to bathe.

In I went, riding my bike past trees, remembering being so much younger, so much smaller so long ago.

At a certain point in the woods, the smell changed. That meant I was getting closer to Dales's "place" if you wanted to call it that. The smell of a vagrant was something you always knew, as the scent changed from green leaves to body odor.

Then I saw him. I both craved for a friend besides Dale and yet was so thankful to have someone to talk to at all in that small hammock of a town. Dale looked so confident, listening to a battery-powered radio I had bought him. I envied him. For despite his homeless situation, he had more confidence – by far – than I did. Dale had a profound understanding of who he was. Anyone who talked to him would not give him a hard time because he looked like he would yell back, while I came across as an easily picked on weakling.

And so it was the reverse: people who did matter didn't, and people who didn't matter did. No matter how fine a person I tried to be, Dale would always seem a higher status to people just because he had a profound understanding of self. Dale was emotionally and mentally healthy. He never, ever came across as confused in any way, such the other way around for me. Again and again, people asked me "Was I all right?"

But I had learned to take it in stride. I got used to being my own best friend, trying to see the advantages of being alone, such as fewer disappointments with people. Then suddenly, as I was riding my bike half daydreaming, Dale spoke:

"James, my man. Come here".

It was such a joy hearing my name called. I rode over. But then he only cared about what I had brought him. I gave Dale a deli sandwich. He looked at me, disappointed and ungrateful, and I hated it when he acted like that.

"What did you want, Dale? A steak dinner?"

And he just laughed in a way that he was indeed laughing at me instead of with me, the same way everyone treated me.

Dale – in 10 years of knowing him, I didn't know his last name – had possibility. I knew he could get a job and get out of the situation he was in, for I saw nothing wrong with Dale medically. Indeed if he joined the military, he could probably be quite a keen soldier.

But Dale had never had any goals, and put no pressure on himself to have them. No foresight to be someone, or motivation to do the mature thing and all that and that and that which people criticized me for had never been on Dale's agenda. Instead, he lived off the land and me, if only because I was the only one big-hearted enough to have supported him much of my youth.

Still, coming to see Dale was an escape from the stressful real world I had to face outside the woods. And indeed I did, again, envy Dale. Life seemed so easy for him; he happy just existing. I wondered what he did all day. With nothing to do, wouldn't he go crazy? I assumed he just listened to that radio as if he were on a cruise, waiting for it to be over and just loafing.

But I was afraid to abandon Dale. I wondered what would happen to him after I left Saturday. Should someone else find out about him, would they have the heart to bring him stuff like I did? I wondered if, just before I left, I should tell someone that there was a homeless man in the woods that needed help. But then Dale might somehow tell my mother I had been supporting him for a decade and so heaven forbid he should be found out.

And so I would just have to hope Dale would be okay. Indeed, he had been in those woods since before I was born, I knowing no more about his past, really, than I knew about Buck's, except that Buck was a lifelong friend of my mother.

Looking at Dale, I realized how true it must be that people didn't change. No one I knew ever did. And I couldn't say much different about myself. Change was painful. And so Dale must find it easier to stay in the same situation: here in the woods, hiding under a tree when it rained without criticism of doing nothing, while I bagged groceries and got criticized for having big, bulging red eyes that came from worrying so much. If that half-shaven man wanted to trade places with me, he could sure cover it up.

Dale looked at me, still wanting more. I gave him a candy bar, wondering again who would help him in the long run when I had moved on from there, at least for a while.

He looked at what I gave him. I sensed un-appreciation. A spoiled vagrant him, never the manners of "thank you." Still, I did not know his childhood. Maybe in fact no one had ever cared about him. Maybe he grew up in an orphanage and never really learned taste and tact from loved ones. Who knew?

He looked at me in a way that everyone else did: as if I was strange. As if I was a snob for some reason because I was not saying anything and because I had a look of strangeness in my different personality; in my being eccentric. And like so many who stuck their noses in the air instead of speaking to me, I knew Dale did not have the nerve to be criticizing me when he had his faults, like living off others.

But that was how Dale was. Like everyone else, he could not see himself. If only he knew the imperfect person he was. But instead he had high self esteem if only, again, because he was mentally healthier than me, despite being a vagrant.

I remembered another Dale, though. One long ago, who seemed to have promise, again, of eventually getting out of the situation he was in. But it was now some ten years later, he not any more far along, living still in the woods, sponging from me.

I noticed something in his pocket. He pulled out a cigarette. It was one of mine! I knew Dale had his faults, though I never imagined him taking my stuff. But it wouldn't do any good to say anything. And indeed he had it hard, with nowhere to live but the woods for as long as I had known him. But still, stealing of any kind was wrong. Somehow though, on that day, I blew it off. Dale would be forever desperate, though I was still mad. And we stood there among the loneliness of the trees, and I watched Dale smoke my cigarette, he looking like he couldn't possibly care less about anything but an escape for free. At least when I looked at yearbooks in my room, I wasn't wrongly taking anything from anyone for pleasure. It was an honest read.

Then, suddenly, Dale walked up to me in the very real sense of being selfishly angry.

"Where were you this morning?" he said with an ignorant voice because I had forgotten to bring him his breakfast doughnut.

"Well, what do you want?," I said. "Maybe you should learn to fend for yourself instead of living off other people."

He just gave a look – a stubborn kind of look – that told me he was really like everyone else I knew, and wasn't going to change. And so I would be the brave one who changed and grew over all the others in my life who didn't because they were scared; because they were lazy. People would find an excuse to stay in the same familiar situation. To keep being how they were instead of feeling something new, different inside themselves: growth.

Then Dale got smart with me.

"My, aren't you the philosopher" he said in a cynical tone, instead of taking responsibility for his middle-aged – and so quite adult – self.

Dale had such a white face as he rarely was out of the woods and in the sun. Why did I bother with him? I had asked myself that question so many times, but always I returned to the routine of sneaking to him food and drinks and cigarettes, which we would smoke together and talk. And so, as the old saying went, things stayed in their place and the empire – the palace of Dale's with his tent site in the woods that is – was maintained.

Dale started manipulating.

"You're not a friend," he said to me, "You're an acquaintance."

I was so hurt. Part of me knew I was just being used so he could continue to get something from me, and I felt I had failed Dale as a friend that day. I didn't know just how to react. I both wanted to kiss his feet and write him off forever. When it came to taking what you could get as far as friendship, Dale and Buck were it in my life.

Dale turned his back to me and started to walk back to his tent site.

"You're not a man. You're still a boy," he grumbled.

"Look at you, he continued. "Still living with your mother and almost nineteen."

That comment stabbed me in the heart. I began to believe then that I was a failure and that Dale, even though he was homeless, was still somehow above me as far as being a real man.

And how could I leave?

I was so attached to Dale and the woods. Addicted to loving the familiarity of the house, the grocery, and the town. How could I leave it all Saturday, even in the name of patriotism? I was one that curled up in the face of the slightest bit of stress, while people like Dale seemed to be able to survive anything. I was so scared and felt so alone as Dale walked farther and farther away from me. And suddenly I felt alone in the woods, feeling like I didn't have a friend in the world. like the world was standing still and I was the only one in it.

I squealed.

"Dale" I said.

"Whaaaat," he yelled back, making fun of my voice.

I ran toward him and I knew he loved it. I realize now that he always knew I would go back to him if only because, like my mother, I had a dependent personality. I hated being alone. I wanted to feel needed, which was the same reason my mother cooked for me every day of my life and why I loved scrubbing the grocery floors for Buck just as much as I hated it.

"Wait right there" I said to Dale at his tent.

And I ran to get him some of my mother's peanut butter, which she had so much of she would not notice that one jar was gone.

As I ran happily, I tried to ignore how sad it was that I had never had anyone but Dale and Buck for friends.

"Go fast" yelled Dale from way behind me where he was standing.

It was a mean thing to say.

8

Having brought Dale his peanut butter, it came time to exit the woods for almost the final time: mom was making dinner; I had things to do. But of course Dale always had something to throw at me.

"Hey, you're your own worst enemy" which, again, he said so I would continue what he wanted, which was to continue to bring him stuff, which he was always afraid I would stop doing.

And I would suddenly pause right there, as I always did, and come back walking quickly toward him, concerned for his well being as well as having human contact outside of that lonely house with my mother.

Then I felt between two points: I was standing in front of Dale, giving him attention, and yet I was distant from him, ready to move on from there Saturday.

Part of me cared about him, and part of me was glad I might never see Dale again in a few days. Indeed certainly never again if I died in war. And yet it was as if Dale and I had both died inside from being rejected by society for so long just because we didn't fit in: he homeless and I without confidence. I had a home and Dale knew who he was and so, like with Buck and I, we wanted a piece of what each other had.

Dale blew smoke from his breath in my face and laughed. While he thought that was funny, I did not. There was such a thing as politeness and tact, and that just was rude. But again, I didn't say a word. Like with Buck, I would keep quiet and let Dale wallow in his misery that he felt deep down, though he could seem happy by the way he came across. It is only now that I realize how deceiving looks can be and how you would never know by looking at people just how scared they are inside.

I pondered my surroundings. So many memories of those woods. Like the steps I often sat on in our house, the trees and woods hadn't changed. But I had. My wants and needs were complex, as I was a creative, deep-thinking person whom people had a hard time understanding, especially in a small area like that one where I had always lived.

I was so sick of it as I continued to look around. And yet it was home. It was familiar.

I just had to see it all as a lesson. There had been a lot of unfairness from being so alone in that house and town all those years, but I was all the better for it. And so I could choose to stand there looking at Dale and whine, or I could be thankful for what - for who - I had. It was up to me. And I had to be the man and act grown up and not cry anymore.

I somehow got a grip on myself and continued to deal with Dale and with my situation at all. I proceeded back out of the woods. But I would never stop worrying about who I was leaving behind.

Toward the beginning of the woods I rode my bike, my secure environment almost gone. Surrounded by the trees and thick brush, I again both loved it and was bored with it. To me, it was the exotic part of the midwest. Beautiful to me because it was home. The only woods I wanted to see. Though I regretted it had never met its potential for development, at least that meant it had stayed quiet. Thus unlike many "boomtowns," at least there were trees not replaced by buildings.

The meteor canyon and the arch hadn't done that. The people of that town had made sure of it. Residents of Fell just wanted tourists to come through, spend money at the grocery and gas station, and move on. Resistance to change was how it went with small towns, but maybe that could be good.

The meteor had cut such a wide gash it was hard to believe there were any woods. But there was a good portion of it. Woods I remembered as fondly as my memories of the rest of the town. They were a wonderful getaway from my stressful routine, consisting of trees that had grown up along with me. I knew it all so well as I rode my bike over the sticks and brush. It spoke to me.

The woods seemed made for men; for those like Dale and I. A woman surely wouldn't feel safe here in a place like the woods, especially by herself. Guys liked to be independent, and I relished that and being alone, deep in thought.

I remembered being in those woods the first day of high school in 9th grade. Everything still seemed the same as then, the situation of boredom bothering me as much as it did then, only now like a candle flame in the wind I was about to be gone, perhaps forgotten by this town as if I were never here. And I wanted to leave my mark on those trees, those woods, that village that had raised me.

Just as I felt the chocolate bars that filled the grocery were like a tomb of unknown soldiers I was soon to be part of, I also felt like those trees: living, but unable to be heard and understood. Emitting life and age, but seen as just happy just existing, seeming to have such an easier life than me because they weren't human. Maybe I would re-incarnate as one of them, such being my karma of having at least a better break in the next life: not having to work or deal with people.

Reaching the beginning of the woods, Dale came running up to me in his tattered and torn clothes:

"What will you do without me Saturday, James? I'll worry about you. What will do without me to keep you company or your mother to take care of you? You see,

James, you're a special guy. A special person with special needs. Like, you appear very young."

What Dale had just said to me was both the worst thing I could hear from someone and yet the best thing. Half the reason Dale had made the statements about my life – that I was "a special guy" with "special needs"- was because, again, I knew very well that he may well have to wait a long, long time before he ever found anyone as big-hearted as me to give him stuff.

Yet on the other half of the stick, knowing Dale had been the only time anyone outside my family – that is, my mother who I had always lived in our house with – had ever really opened up to me (Buck sure didn't). Indeed, for a minute, Dale seemed like a normal friend that I had.

There I was: a footstep away from being in the light out of the woods, which I was avoiding because it was a light that was not happy, and yet behind me – in the darkness – was someone who should be depressing me all the more but instead with his honest words, made my day.

But the gap had already begun building between Dale and I. Though we saw each other almost every day, both of us we're experiencing big life changes: I was about to move on and Dale was about to pass his 60th birthday in three days. Again I thought of Dale's possible, hidden potential. I thought it a shame that Dale would never have the chance to go to college – indeed, I assumed he didn't have an education past third grade – but he again seemed to have such a good mind underneath all that vagrancy and lack of taking a daily shower.

Soon, as I was bicycling alone toward my house, I noticed something as the pebbles crunched under my feel while I walked: Darlene's window was up. I had always seen it locked and closed. I knew it was illegal to be a peeping tom, but I couldn't help but want to sneak over to the window, crouch underneath it, and see what she did off the job when she was at home relaxing.

9

I crouched in the bushes, probably as excited as I have ever been in my life. I had thoughts of success with romance biting at me as much as the summer mosquitos. For once, I wasn't afraid of getting in trouble. And for that, I was proud of myself.

Everything changed when, trying as hard as I could to not be seen, I peered in Darlene's window. What I saw was, to me, absolutely not happening.

She was crying.

Crying in front of her makeup mirror, bawling to herself with statements like "why can't I be a Marie Curie instead of a grocery store cashier? Why didn't I go to college? Why am I only seen for my looks and not my brains?"

I was dumbfounded. Here was the same woman — whom I so much loved — that always seemed so cheerful and fearless and emotionally and mentally healthy at work. The woman that could light up my world on days when Buck was not in a good mood and took it out on me.

I wanted so much to comfort her, but how could I? She might not at all like a peeping Tom, even if she worked with him. And so I could only watch.

And Darlene continued to cry while sitting in front of the mirror. And I thought I was the only one who had problems. I shamed myself.

Suddenly I began to see that everyone had something to deal with; I just stood out, gave a negative vibe, looked 12 years old no matter how old I got.

But I couldn't see why Darlene was crying. She had everything she could want, at least when it came to looks. She came across with a confidence that would cause no one to dare give her a hard time.

Why did Darlene's husband leave her? It was such a mystery, for she was strikingly beautiful all right. It made the town – divided by a meteor that crashed – all the more a mystery. Something must have happened to Darlene – and the town – that I did not yet know about, but might unlock answers to knowing myself.

I had known Darlene and Buck all my life. Indeed they had always been the only ones that ever came to my birthday parties. But they both seemed so full of secrets. I had always sensed such. And my mother was always afraid of me saying anything that would offend either of them as my mother, Darlene and Buck were lifelong friends.

Then for a minute everything was silent. It was, again, like I was on an island alone as I crouched under the window. Indeed what I was feeling was not far from dying and seeing my life pass before me. I felt that much of an adrenaline rush.

Then I was caught between two possibilities: knocking on Darlene's door or going home for dinner. I knew my mother would be mad if I were late and my food sat on the table, getting cold. And yet, this was my moment to be in the house with the woman I loved. To me, such would be as good as carrying Darlene over the threshold on our honeymoon, even if the honeymoon of my fantasies.

I eyed the front door. It had a small sign on it that said "Welcome" and below that "Peace to all who enter here." And indeed Darlene's property was peaceful, and I did feel welcome, even if I was still standing – crouching – outside the house. But even if she did invite me in, I would know Darlene was now a very different, very real person of which I had never realized before. Darlene was very, very sad on the inside. She had wanted to be a professor, I could see, and she hadn't dared to attempt the schooling and pressure it required.

Could I help her? Indeed I could hardly help myself. But I wanted to be a part of Darlene's life. She was, again, the fairest of them all. Her looks. Her voice. Her entire disposition just blew you away with its charm. I wondered if she realized her looks could have gotten her a professor's job. For indeed, that was how she had gotten the grocery cashier position. Indeed, I thought, there in the bushes, Darlene could get almost anything she wanted because of her looks.

But maybe that was part of why I loved Darlene: because we were so opposite: people took her seriously, and at the same time, pretended like I didn't exist. And yet we were alike in that people judged us from our outsides – her with her looks and me with my young face – and yet on the inside, we were both very intelligent. Far, far smarter than we thought we were.

I got up out of the bushes, and though I was scared to death I knew I might never get this close to going inside ever again. I walked up to the door and it seemed, now, like I was the entire universe, master of everything, James the god of all gods standing there shaking.

A combination of adrenaline and fear was rushing through me as I knocked on Darlene's front door and waited for her to answer. I felt like I had been waiting for this chance all my life. Indeed, I had never in my life been inside Darlene's house. I felt like a begging vacuum cleaner salesman as I had not done the polite thing and phoned her that I was coming. Would she be welcoming? After all, she had just been crying. And so what mood would she show, happy or sad? Though around others Darlene of course had always worn a smile, I knew now it was not always a real one.

I did not look all that presentable, which I indeed regretted. I had been sweating for spying out in the hot

August sun and my work shoes made my feet feel sore as it had been a long day bagging groceries. But I knew Darlene could look beyond that, as she always seemed to look for the best in people: even though people did not see the academic potential she wanted to be seen on her inside, she tried to like people for their heart within. Darlene had so much love inside her and I knew that, even if she were surprised to see me at her door, she would be kind and welcoming.

When she opened the door, it was almost like an earthquake. That's how shaken up I was with excitement when we looked at each other. Though I now knew her look of confidence was not real, I still wanted to believe it was genuine and that for the moment, as I stood there outside her door, she knew I existed. Would she take me seriously? The whole thing was my fantasy when it came to her and I.

"What do you need?" she said, surprised.

I didn't know what to say, and then she said:

"Well come in, come in" in the most gracious way.

I followed her into the living room, looking around at all her beautiful furniture, the house immaculate, not a sign of dust.

She sat down quickly on the couch, ushering me with her eyes to do the same and so I did, this being the first time she might truly open up to me. I wanted to kiss her but she gestured not to, pushing me away with her beautiful hand on my chest. But it was still lucky to get so close and intimate with her at all.

"Do you want something to drink?" she said cheerfully, to all the more to wean me away from wanting to grab her and kiss her on the couch.

"Sure," I said.

"And thanks."

As women were, Darlene said everything so gracious and genuine and it made me feel so good. Why was it, I thought, that females were better with people than males? I knew if I visited Buck's house, he would likely not be so welcoming although, ironically, I had to be nice when he was about to "visit" me.

I watched her as she strode into the kitchen, her long blonde hair twirling all over on top of her oh so fair figure. Even just the back of her was enough to please any man. Then she turned around and with her hand, motioned me to follow her. I was so excited. I had never seen the kitchen- indeed not even this house at all – of this woman I would always love, even if she were well old enough to be my mother.

It was so happy, she and I in the kitchen as I held the glass and she poured delicious pink lemonade into it. It tasted so good; it would probably be the most delicious drink I would ever taste, as soon I would have to go back outside into a world that criticized. A world that essentially served lemonade that was particularly bad. But in here with Darlene, fantasy reigned. Me away from my problems, if only for a very short time.

Before I knew it, time flew. I was enjoying myself that much – the joy of companionship with this woman I loved – even if she was just a friend. And yet I refused to see her as just that. To me, Darlene would never be just a friend or acquaintance or, soon, "part of my past." She was what kept me going. I wanted her to notice me flexing my muscles, not having a twelve-year-old looking face at almost nineteen. But the fact was I didn't have any muscles to show off. I was small and skinny, just the opposite of my mother and most of my relatives that had been born "big-boned." And I had seen pictures of my late father, he a big well built guy, anything but skinny. Why did that bother me? Why did I keep questioning my worth? Why was I a perfectionist, so hard on myself?

I wanted a lot of things to happen that very moment and not later if ever it really would anyway. I wanted our little lemonade party in the kitchen to turn romantic enough to become a marriage proposal. But it was to no avail. I knew I would never get any farther with her than having this lemonade. Still, for some reason, I couldn't give up.

I daydreamed for a moment as we stood there. I saw myself in a tuxedo and my love was wearing a wedding gown and we were marching down one of the grocery aisles as weddings in Fell were always held at the grocery, as were many town events. And Buck was my best man. It was so special, for my dream of marrying Darlene to have come true.

Then my daydreaming flashed beyond that, and Darlene and I were on vacation to St. Louis, which to both of us was as far away as our lives could get. It was the other side of the world to us and anyone else living in Fell. And we were staying at a nice hotel that overlooked the arch, which we were going to pay to take a ride on that day.

And finally my dreams flashed ahead one more time, and Darlene and I were in a nursing home, having spent a wonderful life together.

Then, suddenly, I snapped out of my dream and was back where I wanted to stay forever. But both our glasses of lemonade were almost empty, and I knew Darlene and I both had to get up early for work tomorrow.

Darlene yawned, hinting that I shouldn't wear out my welcome, though more than anything in the world I wanted to. Indeed I wanted to move in the same day. I wanted to offer to be her butler for free room and board. But instead we both walked toward the front door and I stepped outside it, back to the beginning of the rainbow.

10

It was like I was alone in a desert. Everything around – and inside me – barren. I imagined seeing the mirage that rose from the sands: my moment of hopeful romance with Darlene. And then, like the Salem witchcraft hysteria, it ended as quickly as it began. No closer was I to owning Darlene or any other woman. Instead, I was just plain old James, supposed to be proud that I would be joining Uncle Sam and giving him what he wanted, yet in a way pride not fully felt as I was not happy having not gotten my piece of the pie, the one called love and marriage and kiddies. All that, I knew, may forever elude me unless I settled for someone I didn't want, like Penelope, and how could I marry my cousin, whom I had also with little choice gone to the prom with?

I looked down. The pebbles covered a wide area from Darlene's house to everything you could see from there. More pebbles than you had ever seen in your life. And I was both sick of them and loved them. Loved them for their familiarity, and my little game I carried into my adulthood that the pebbles were aliens talking to me, something that to this day made me less lonely and something as to which I needed to grow up and now abandon, as traditions had to end. Boys had to become men.

I would always think about the pebbles and my day in Darlene's house. I was glad for such memories, as I knew they could never be the same anywhere else in my life again. Nowhere would ever be like here in Fell. A place I had lived a lifetime.

Things should have been spinning. That is, I should have been tipsy while standing outside there in the night. But the fact was I didn't have a beer or two with Darlene. Instead, I was Mr. Goody Two Shoes who just enjoyed lemonade, having never drunk, had never smoked an illegal substance like pot or had pre-marital sex. But those were choices that made me happy, though such came with a heavy price: I didn't get invited anywhere and those I loved, like Darlene, didn't take me seriously – didn't open up to me - because I wouldn't do naughty things everyone else did, aside from an occasional smoke.

The truth was, I was scared of what having sex would be like. I was afraid it would hurt, though only Penelope knew that about me as she seemed so easy anyway with her awful freckles, and so what did it matter if I told her my secrets? Penelope said I should talk to a sex doctor about it, but the truth was I would rather die, plus they might want a lot of money. Maybe having sex with a woman would have made me happier? I didn't know. I'd never known it. I was just a lonely, searching country boy from Fell, Missouri who, like everyone else, blamed his problems on things outside himself.

Always I wanted to stop time. Always I didn't want to budge from where I was sitting or standing when I was deep in thought, away from my problems by daydreaming. But like an astronaut returning from outer space, eventually I had to face reality and people who weren't nice and then more people who weren't nice.

Why was it looked down upon not to get a girl pregnant? Why were people praised for messing up? Was it more moral 100 years ago? Or had it been and would it always be that bad people had more friends because people liked the element of risk? How could I win? I guess I really was just a perfectionist then, playing a game with myself I could never win, like Amelia Earhart, she a woman so far ahead of others. Ahead of her time. And I was ahead of that town that I couldn't help but love if only because I knew it.

I wanted to be standing outside her house there kissing Darlene, though I didn't know how to kiss properly. And it would be something I would want Jamie to see so he would be jealous, though he would be master at covering it up.

As I stood there, I pretended to be kissing. That I didn't want anyone to see, but I did it right out in the open anyway. Kissing an invisible Darlene was better than no Darlene. Kissey. Kissey. Smooch Smooch. Her lipstick on me. It made me look like such a naughty boy and I loved it.

I sat on the ground. My fantasy was over. I had to deal with being by myself. Making my own parade. Laughing to myself and I had fun that way.

I needed to get home for dinner. And while I was so sick of that same routine, I also realized that I might never eat there again come Saturday. No telling who would survive the battlefield and who, out of bravery for their country, wouldn't. Did I wish it would be me that didn't live? No. I loved life too much. Still, surviving would mean I would have the guilt of living when so many others didn't tacked on to all that people already gave me a hard time about.

I knew military people were going to be people. Just a different breed, nice and mean. What should I tell them when they asked me if I had a girlfriend, which they inevitably would, just as much as people here at home asked? I knew I could lie and say yes, but then you get into the habit of lying and can't stop. And that wasn't me. I'd always, absolutely always told the truth even if, like most people, I was full of secrets.

And so it all was, and so I thought about facing reality standing alone in the night in front of my dream girl's house, having gotten a small escape from my problems. Having had a normal friend for a minute twice in a day.

11

I sat on the bench on my break. I thought of things to come. Of the army bus.

I had seen it. Nothing fancy, paint of army green. The bus was nice, from what I had heard. There wasn't that of trains - dining car — but better, perhaps, than an uncomfortable, long sailing on a ship, where I might get seasick.

But the worst of it all: the anticipation. Wouldn't be as scary once in it. I could only guess its actual way. The bus driver, it's said, gets out and salutes, then I get on. That's how it's done – bus driver in full military uniform. I dressed nice and ready as I would ever be, on to the bus. Excited.

A new venture.

Through tourist traffic it'd go, the driver keeping pace confidently. Residents would wave, honk for us, for either way it would go with our lives. Then the bus would trail through Missouri for Virginia. I would sit in front, as I always had on the school bus. Trip long, but time always goes by so quickly.

The bus would stop for a break. Door opening, young excited faces pouring out.

Oh, good times and hardship our lives would be daily.

And Jamie would twirl his racket as I first got on, leaving him behind. I would look at his eyes for maybe the last time. His look would bug me - holding power - and then, like a flash of light, gone.

And so there was me sitting there on the bench trying to predict what it would be like and then, of course, it happening and it not being like I thought.

By the time the bus passed through the town limits and approached the Missouri state line, I would begin to feel more and more what I had given up for what was coming. The bus would park at its final destination, and I would gather my things and step down from the bus and into the barracks, the great base ablaze in military green. I, of course, still feeling the same insecurities.

They weren't, I kept realistically reminding myself, going away just because I was in a new place.

12

Almost time to clock back in. I sat on the bench. A tour bus drove by and stopped at the grocery entrance. The tourists got off. Excited faces.

The bus driver was excited too, I could tell, about seeing that arch. I had seen the scenario so many times. Excited over nothing.

As he spoke to the bus driver Buck looked at his watch to seem important, busy, and compare his job with what he saw as the more menial job of the bus driver, being a snob as he talked about having worked there since he was 12 years old, his father having owned it. I knew he was talking about that. Always that subject with bus drivers. His job above theirs. Bragging. But how did one change someone else? I accepted my boss. Would soon accept him as step-dad.

The huge vehicle disappeared into the road to St.Louis, it again the big city to us small towners. I never really got an exciting, far away vacation, so I didn't understand the perspectives of many of those I bagged for taking it.

Needed to clock in, yet remained on the bench. My obsessive thoughts repeated: studying Darlene's movements through the glass of the grocery a few yards away. She slim, tall, a heck of a good looking female, even if middle-aged. Despite a slight sideways walk in her back, she was just beautiful, able to socialize. Clothes always seemed to fit her: not too rich or poor, as if polite as possible. Oh, just the kind you wanted around. Hair long and blonde, despite it colored. She stood at the register, energy-filled, looking to be doing it just right. I never wanted to handle money. But she brave, accurate with it. No airhead; concentration keen.

Yet unfortunately I had seen the real, crying Darlene, she really feeling her beauty worked against her, making men feel she was so beautiful she could not be pleased with any man, making men feel lower than her, figuring she was married or had many boyfriends, both not true, instead never getting asked out because of those assumptions. She looked at her watch, a busy schedule outside of work, giving older adults she knew at church a ride somewhere. She was always doing for others; I knew, despite her well-hidden insecurities, she liked to take care of people.

I threw bread to the birds. Through the glass again, Buck and Darlene talking, he never giving her a hard time. I wished I could be like them, like others. Why did Buck seem to insult only me? Buck walked outside and brought in carts. He short and fat, wearing a nice shirt. His face round, business looking, emotionless.

Buck shook Jamie's hand, and in a way never with me. It was with respect, despite I working full time and Jamie not at all.

I walked toward the grocery. Neither said hi. I smelled Buck's cologne, he divorced, hoping to seem sexy for the ladies. He was lonely, but master at covering it up, while I as to it a dead giveaway, people constantly judging my facial contortions.

"Are you ready for work, boy?" Buck said as I was halfway through the door.

Men liked tearing each other apart.

"Ready as I'll ever be" was all I said.

Always same in conversation, Buck only thinking about work, business. The truth was he had little in life as to people, friends for like me, he didn't mix. We both just lived for our grocery work.

13

I again thought of being there in in the presence of Darlene as I bagged, altogether a comforting sight to please any man, one that shot through me with that rush of adrenaline. Had I not seen her crying the night before, I never would have guessed she was not happy with men not loving the real her, but instead just her looks. She wanted them to see her Marie Curie. She knew she could have been Dr. Darlene something by now. A scientist. Something like that. But no, she had chosen this. The grocery, the head cashier position. If only because it was less stress because of less pay, among other things. She would have to put in long hours as a professor. Publish or perish, as she must have heard they had to do. She did not want that responsibility. And yet she was not happy where she presently was, deep down, either.

And so she continued with looking confident, always with a face that could light up the world. No sign of pain and hardship in her. In her expression, there was no hint of sadness, perhaps though being able to cover it up – bottle it up – made it all the worse for her. She wanted people to see her as the way she was – scared – but she loved the attention she got from being able to hide it. And so she lived a sort of double life, a sort of Miss America on the outside and Miss Insecure on the inside. It made her tired.

I studied her.

I realized she did not have the nerve to tell me she only liked me as a friend, even though I had worked together closely with her at the grocery for three years. She and the whole grocery were comfortable to me if only because I had never really known anything else. And so I didn't care what was "out there" in the big wide world because I had never seen it.

And so things in my life were not as they seemed: Darlene was not as happy as she came across; I was luckier than I thought I was to have had stability from always living in the same house in the same town. It must just have been human nature not to be satisfied. Or maybe simply Darlene and I were too intellectual for that small enclave of a town?

I was beginning to find out quite a few things about the real her, and in that, the real me. From then on, I would question that woman's confident demeanor. A pretend demeanor that I had not known was so for a lifetime.

But even though I now knew there was a much different, much unhappy Darlene on the inside, I still loved that woman. She still kept me going through depressing, lonely days. She still was part of my brightest and happiest memories, first from knowing her as a life-long friend of my mother growing up and then getting to work with her at the grocery. I knew she would never do anything like move away. I knew she couldn't do that. There were too many memories for her to leave.

And so for once I didn't want Darlene's great life or her confidence since both didn't exist. And it had taken me so long to realize that. I had to see her secretly in tears to even know. What a way to find out about someone's "real" way. She was frightened. And she wanted to pour it out in admitting to it: to being unhappy. It was convenient for her to turn to help someone else, thus me at the moment. And so continued her now-I-knew-phony nurturing:

"You made it through high school. How does that make you feel?"

I knew she would say that. She and the town were now becoming so predictable. But I figured anyone could get a high school diploma. It wasn't much of a victory. After all, I was one of thousands - millions - who got it.

Darlene's face twisted into a fun, painted grin. It was a look that lighted up my world from the confidence that was not sincere. Boy could that woman be an actress.

And yet I would continue to go on feeling sincerely comfortable with her presence. I would keep loving her. Dreaming about Darlene all the time, clinging to the hope that this insecure woman would fall madly in love with me, though I offered little in the way of confidence myself.

Now that I knew the real Darlene, the atmosphere on the grocery floor between us was frustratingly tense. There was heavy silence. I gave a frustrated smile, asking myself, How could Darlene and I help or love each other when we couldn't do either for ourselves?

14

I waited to bag groceries, as there were no customers. But I knew it would not stay that way. Soon a tour bus would surely pull up and the masses would pour in, always buying so much candy for their vacations.

Darlene spoke to me as we stood there in the quiet, Buck in the office doing whatever:

"Does Buck bother you?," Darlene said in a kind tone.

"Don't let him get to you," she continued, "his bark is worse than his bite."

I was surprised that Darlene would say that, for if Buck knew, couldn't it cause problems with her job? And I didn't know how to respond. I was afraid for both of us: Darlene needed the job to pay her bills and I needed it for a reference, not to mention I wanted to come back here again someday and work in it the rest of my life though, again, I knew deep down Buck would hate to see me own and manage it.

"Yeah, yeah" I said in a teenager sort of way.

And Darlene laughed. She and I had known Buck for so long that we could predict him: his mood swings; the fact that he was not going to change; his greediness. Things everyone who came to know Buck eventually realized about him, had to accept him for.

"I want to know how it goes for you in the army, James," Darlene then said.

"Be sure to visit us when you are home."

She didn't know home would be the storeroom.

I knew that Buck knew I did more work than anyone else at the grocery. Indeed I broke my back for him and the customers. If not for me, I knew the grocery would not be so well done. Or at least Buck would have to do it all himself because he would never find an employee as good as me.

Sometimes we were so short of help, I did not get to take a break. And when I questioned him about taking one, Buck would say "we'll talk about it a little later."

But I was thankful: thankful to have a job, not to mention the one of my dreams.

Later in the day, it slowed down again and Darlene and I once again chatted at the register:

"So, what kinds of things do you like to do, James, aside from work I mean?"

I paused. I would feel funny letting Darlene know there was nothing in my life but work and looking at school yearbooks. And then came the question I dreaded:

"Do you have a girlfriend?" she said.

"No" I said blushing.

"I understand, James" she said.

I appreciated that. I hated that question. Why did you have to have a significant other or be married and have kids? Wasn't it ok to be alone? Why couldn't people mind their own business? And yet it meant at least that people were interested in my life. It was better than being ignored.

"After work, I sometimes go riding my bike in the woods" I said, which was true, even if it was to go feed the homeless man to have someone to talk to sometimes.

"Oh, I love the woods too, James. I had part of my wedding there, by the pond. It's where someone threw the bouquet."

I knew about that because Darlene had talked about it so many times. Beautiful as she was, Darlene's marriage had not worked out, which was surprising because she was again a woman of astounding beauty, both inside and out. She could surely have won any beauty contest she entered. She was as good at being beautiful as my mother was at gobbling down peanut butter.

I had heard her talk about her ex-husband, he having dropped out of college at the University of Missouri and so Darlene wondered if he could then stay with anything. And then, soon after the honeymoon, they divorced, which Darlene said was something you could see coming.

"But it was still painful," she had said.

"Divorce is the worst thing that can happen to a person."

Jamie came out of the office.

"How is the homeless man?" he said to me shockingly.

"How did you know about him?" I said, really scared that someone had found out.

"I saw you bringing him food yesterday."

I cautioned Jamie to talk a little quieter as we stood away from the register for a few minutes.

"Jamie, please don't tell anyone I'm feeding him. My mother would have a cow."

"Ok, ok, James" Jamie said looking around, embarrassed to be seen with me.

It was no longer a secret. The cat was out of the bag about Dale. I would, from then on, have to be extra nice to Jamie all the time, or he would tell. It made me all the more glad to be getting out of the State of Missouri entirely in a few days, and yet I had to worry about what Jamie would say about me to whoever when I was gone. It had been a secret for so long it had started not to matter. But now I was essentially the slave of Buck and now also Jamie.

Somehow I managed to do a pretty good job of finishing out my shift bagging groceries that day. I dealt with my situation. Dwelt on it too much and I would go crazy.

"Why can't I trade places with someone else Darlene?" I said to her.

Darlene was shocked by that.

"You're fine James," she said,

"I wish I were in your shoes," she continued. "You have a mother to cook and clean for you. I have to do all that myself."

"Oh, I would give anything to be anyone but me" I said.

Then Darlene didn't want to hear my problems.

"You said that yesterday" she said, motioning to me that we both needed to be working as the store was getting busy again.

I had a way of doing that with people: telling them my problems, which my mother said people didn't want to hear. And it hurt when I even got on Darlene's nerves, as she seemed more patient and nurturing than even my mother.

And so I backed away, tried to do what I had to do at the grocery quietly, trying to realize that bitterness was not a desirable trait.

"Are you attracted to me Darlene?" I said to her as she was busily doing the register.

"Honey," she said gruffly. And I knew then I better leave her alone; quit while I was ahead for the rest of that workday.

Again and again it happened: a window of hope seemed to be opening – Darlene falling in love with me, Buck having respect for me, Jamie not standing there bragging about his tennis victories as I bag – but then all those things reversed.

In a way, my mother had already kicked me out. It as if I was already living in the grocery basement storeroom, as if there was already a mattress in it. When in the storeroom, ever those boxes of chocolate bars seeming to greet me like a tomb of unknown soldiers, of whom I was next to be buried with. I could almost hear the patriotic music that blared through the grocery changing into funeral music, indeed the very kind for fallen soldiers.

"Good luck in whatever you do in life" Darlene said to me.

I was bothered by that. What did that mean? Was she glad to be getting rid of me or something? Indeed I was just too sensitive. But everything Darlene said to me gave me hope of romance with her, and then she would go back to doing the register again, and the hope of love and romance would once again dry up. I only kept hoping for a date with her because it got me through the day, sort of like with laughter.

15

___

Next day. Work. All were there: Buck, Darlene, and Jamie with his tennis racket. They looked at me. Unsure. Who was that man?

"He's almost to leave for the army" said Darlene.

I blushed. The roller coaster of love hopes to me from that woman. Always it seemed just a trip downward. Maybe someday it would be different.

Like I had once heard, "vision never allows you to accept anything that is negative."

And if I visualized enough of "Darlene loving me," would it maybe happen? Of course not. Then you could keep visualizing winning contest numbers and eventually win with them. Money and love, for me at least, would always rarely come easily.

"Good luck, Mr. Soldier" she said, sounding nurturing to cover up the sadness that I now knew was inside her.

But again, though fake, I loved her. Splendid figure. Blonde hair. Just the most beautiful woman I had ever seen. It was impossible not to fall in love with her.

Then, end of the little party of hopes, Buck coming out of the office. He takes my arm. Gently pushes me away from daydreaming on the clock and to be working, it toward his own gain. The grocery his factory. His empire until his dying day, he surely afraid to retire and grow old with the pain of watching someone else have it. Yes, that man would work until he died. Just another of Buck's ways. Indeed it might as well be called "Buck's Grocery." And who knew? Maybe that was what would be in his will, along with all he would get from my mother's.

Always Buck and I trying to get closer to something: I to the last day of work at the grocery for a while and Buck to my mother's will, neither of us patient. Instead, we got back at each other suttle: facial grimaces; gossip behind each other backs. But always he had the upper hand, just like a teacher. Indeed working at the grocery often felt like school. The same grind, always seeming to take more than it gave. Still, I was making money. And I liked to do that. I liked that steady paycheck, which I knew would be even bigger coming from the military, but still my heart was here.

Clocking out for a nice thirty-minute rest, I surveyed the grocery, mentally grabbing all the memories I could. Sentimentally. Before one knew it, the Christmas holidays would have arrived. I wondered what it would be like if I came to visit then? There wouldn't be room for me to sleep amidst all those soup cans. But then I would never be allowed to sleep there ever again after what was to happen. My "guest room" would be the grocery basement storeroom forever when it came to being home on my breaks.

Later, at the time clock punching back in, I heard Darlene and Buck talking at the register, trying to talk in a tone low enough that I could not hear them:

"He's okay, Buck" said Darlene asking Buck why he was trying to get me to quit and go in the military, Buck just looking as if not knowing how to act when confronted about it.

Buck said to Darlene, "you look nice today."

Darlene gave him a womanly complaint:

"It's awfully hot in here"

"I knew you were going to say that" said Buck.

"Well, why are you too cheap to run the air conditioner?"

I tried to control my laughing. Darlene could roll her eyes and get away with stuff. If I had said that, I figured I might well be out of a job.

"Thanks," said Buck, "I only work 60 hours a week supervising this place and hardly ever have time for myself."

"Remember what we discussed at James's birthday party? When James was in his room as if he had a paper bag over his head?" said Darlene.

I looked at both of them as I stood there at the timeclock. I thought this was going to be the moment of truth, when Buck would turn to me with respect, but no.

"I'm not harsh" Buck said to Darlene.

Lying to himself really, he believing he was the generous employer rather than the slave-driver one.

"Why do you act as if him going in the military is my fault?" said Buck in defense of himself.

Darlene was quick to retort, knowing at the same time she had a job to protect. But for once, she spoke her mind to Buck.

"I don't like how you are influencing him to think that way. What his mother must be saying about you brainwashing she and him to believe soldierhood is the only way he should go" said Darlene.

But Buck only cared about Real Estate.

Again I thought of what my mother had said to me as to Buck:

"I'm sorry if you have issues with Buck at work, but he is an old childhood friend, and so you'll just have to deal with it. If anything happened between us, I don't know what I would do."

And so I just stared at Buck emotionless. And in doing so, it gave Buck yet another excuse to give me a hard time, hearing him talk about me to Darlene:

"In heavens name" Buck said to Darlene, "where did James learn to glare at someone like that? I dedicated all the time I could to going to James's birthday parties and working on car parts with him in the yard, just so James and I could have the kind of father-son relationship neither of us ever got to have truly."

Buck was so full of it. But who else did I have to talk to on that lonely road besides he and Dale?

16

I walked over to the ladder, humble.

"I'll hold the ladder the best I can Buck" I said.

Buck was in one of his moods again and sneered as to whether I could handle it. Why did Buck have to be that way? At times he could be so fun.

I disposed of the bad bulb and went back to bagging. Buck would not relent. He continued to give me pointers on how to bag better.

"The heavy stuff and then the light stuff on top" said Buck.

I did not need to be told that. I knew how to do my job.

"OKAY, Mr. Mellon" I said loudly.

I did not like a confrontation and said no more. Buck was surprised by the comeback but did not want to appear bothered by it.

Then he said, "James, you bag very well but you need to have more confidence."

"I think I am confident" I said.

"I hear you will have the house to yourself the next few nights as it's your mothers week for the peanut butter eating contest?"

"Yes. I am looking forward to it."

"You will have to take care of yourself. Can you handle it?"

"Well, I think I can. I'm almost 19."

I knew Buck wanted to find out all about me being alone that week, but I just let it go in one ear and out the other.

"I shall look forward to the rest."

Buck couldn't keep his big mouth shut.

"You will need people to keep you company,"

I knew I could decide that. Buck pushed harder.

"You might see the likes of me dropping in. I might even cook for you".

How nice, I thought, of Buck to invite himself to be a chef.

I knew what was happening. And as usual, I didn't say a single word about it.

That was tact, and I was going to have tact, even if Buck never did.

"It may not be good for you to be in that house all alone," said Buck, "I mean a week is a long time to be alone in it."

"THANK YOU, MR MELLON" I said loudly.

"Anytime, anytime," said Buck, realizing he had said enough.

I knew all this was for a purpose. To Buck, it was a long and exciting journey that was about to have an explosive ending. And oh, if I only knew how that end was going to be.

I looked at Buck. His eyes told everything about him. The eyes did tell everything about a person. Buck was a con-artist and his eyes glowed like one.

So Buck was going to get the house. So what? What did it matter? I knew I might, if I died in war, of course never come back. So why should I have been bothered by it? Buck was going to do me in somehow, but no one ever said life was fair. I gave Buck a look as if it did not matter anymore what was said between us. Because, for some reason, we were lifelong best friends, even if 30 years apart.

"I have many things here you could use for dinner during your week alone."

Darlene rolled her eyes. Buck always talked about this. Only now, it was just a few days away.

"Yes sir," I said, wondering why I bothered just to let Buck have his way.

"You've told me many times what I could use that we sell here."

Darlene mentioned how she had many fond memories of me as a small child. I was touched and excited. Still, I knew she was not attracted to me.

The look on her face seemed to say: "God be with you child."

I wanted to say to her "you need me. you need me."

Then Buck put in his two cents worth:

"Plus," Buck ranted, "I have chef skills. I could recommend you some good cookbooks."

I didn't know what to say to that. From beginning to end that suggestion was filled with manipulation.

"I don't want you alone in that house a whole week – I want someone to keep you company so they can take care of you,"

Buck didn't have to have said that. He could have kept his mouth shut, but he hadn't. He just wanted total control of me.

"Thanks, Buck." That was all I knew to say regarding that sick trick.

Buck was saying two things. There were "sub-words" underneath what he said. In other words, he might as well have been saying, "I want total control of you and have no respect for you. I want your house."

It was true that with guys it was all about the money.

Buck paused. "I know you aren't a kid anymore, but sometimes we still need help."

"True" I said, once again agreeing because it was easiest.

I did not want to start a confrontation EVER.

Why though, I thought to myself, was I the only one Buck ever said such to?

"To sum it up, you are special," said Buck.

"You're 18, but you just aren't like everybody else."

Just what Dale said.

My blood boiled.

"You know how to make a man feel good about himself" I said cynically.

Buck continued ranting selfishly.

"Don't mention it. Regarding cookbooks again, in the back right corner of the store I have some cookbooks for sale. Since you've done such a good job in the past three years, I'll give you one."

What was I supposed to say? I could not say no.

"Thank you, sir" I said like a robot.

Buck was desperate for that house. He certainly wasn't nice for nothing.

But at the same time I still wanted to believe, deep down, that maybe Buck could be a friend. That maybe he was looking forward to me being his stepson, even if from a distance as soon I would be several states away.

But that wasn't how it was. Buck was out to get something or he would never, I knew, give me even the time of day. He had used me to find out what my mothers favorite chocolate was, which he was glad to have to be able to complement her peanut butter eating.

My mother had long talked of wanting a hard to find european chocolate and so Buck filled the grocery basement storeroom with just that: boxes of her favorite chocolate that had always reminded me of the same thing for three years: a tomb of unknown soldiers of which I seemed next in line for, soon to be sleeping next to them in the storeroom.

It was as if the boxes of chocolate bars had ears; as if they were dead soldiers listening to everything I said and, like is said about aliens, could read my thoughts and communicate with me telepathically too.

I had to get out of that town. And yet it was home.

17

Walking down to the grocery basement storeroom to get some soup cans, there they were.

Always I fantasized about the chocolate bars coming to life - as a former tomb of unknown soldiers rescuing me – with chocolate guns – from my misery and problems by shooting at my enemies. But instead the chocolate bars would only stay just that and increase after I left, sure to spill over into my soon former bedroom next door which was also to be full, I knew, with soup cans, the second biggest item Buck ordered.

But what could I do about it anyway? Buck had the upper hand as my boss and soon as my stepfather, sure to have total control over my gullible mother if he had not always had control anyway, what was going to happen being just a continuation of what had been already going on since the day I was born. Like people born into wealth and privilege and thus never having to worry about money, I was born into circumstance: born in a town with a house next to what seemed like the most politicized grocery in the world.

And I had always known I was destined to one day grow up and work in it and then sleep in it, which I was just about to do. And with those two happenings, the final family shakedown between me, my mother and my almost to be stepfather, Buck Walter Mellon Jr.

Break time in the employee breakroom. A nice long hour, meaning so much. Close my eyes. For a brief time the job is a world away, as are all my problems as I sit in a comfy chair and close my eyes. Such a good feeling to work, but great to rest too. I could complain. But what good would it do? So what if I'll soon live in a storeroom? It could be worse.

It was counting down: just a little while longer and it may well be as if I had never been here. Almost the last time in this breakroom, like when it was the last day of ever being in the high school cafeteria. Passages.

But many things had not passed. I still dwelled on disappointments. The fact that my only date had been the prom with Penelope, if only because no one else would go with either of us.

Still, I was happy. Or maybe just as happy as I made up my mind to be without lying to myself. I didn't know. But maybe if I smiled, it might light up someones else life — someone else's day.

My break time was going by so fast. It was because I didn't want it to end. I wanted to stop time and never grow any older. Indeed I wanted to go back to the childhood innocence of a year and two months ago when I wore that high school cap and gown and all the time before that. I don't know why I would want to go back to my terrible childhood, and childhood was such. I guess it's because I would be returning to familiar territory.

Were people in a small town like island people? Maybe to a degree that might be true, I figured, for I had heard that people on islands were mean. And you were stuck, seeing the same people every day, so you had to get along with them. And so I was glad I had my car and so could get away to St. Louis, the only other side of the world to me.

Perhaps some might think it too bad indeed that almost the only other place I had ever been was St. Louis, born there. I got excited every time I went — the mall, the big city library and the night time with the clubs, which I did go to myself. But it was still a nice getaway. It always had been.

I remembered a different St. Louis I used to visit. Or perhaps a very young, very different me seeing the world with fresh eyes. The St. Louis arch being something I couldn't wait to ride when my mother and I would go to St. Louis to go shopping, loving the bumpy elevator ride from the beginning of the arch to up and over and down the other side. And of course there's a gift shop, but locals of course always pass that by, knowing we could visit anytime.

Life could be far more difficult for me without tourists on the way to that arch who stop in the grocery to buy candy and stuff.

Indeed it had created a job for me, a job that was my life. That I wanted again someday, I hoping to do it then for the rest of my days. Like Buck, I got so much out of working I could do it until I died.

And so a meteor hit where I was born, and tourism from it and an arch fueled my job I grew up dreaming to have one day. And yes I could blame my problems on all those easily said "circumstances" outside myself, or I could be a man and not whine, realizing it was the same situation wherever. I did, though, dream of exotic and exciting places for I had never, ever been past just going to cultural events in the next big city.

Maybe you did make your own excitement. Maybe I hadn't worked hard enough at carving a life for myself here. Did I not give people enough of a chance? Or myself enough of one to brave being truly confident?

What was brave? What was taking chances? Did it matter that I might never go to Hollywood and try to be a star? I supposed that something like that, that "Hollywood" glamour, might be great in the beginning. But then it would start to get old, to wear thin and I would long for another peaceful Missouri summer, Missouri being where I had spent all my summers.

I just had to hope that going in the army was the mature thing to do, even if I was doing it just because of one person. One person who wanted something and would soon be related to me. All that being things that were in my nightmares, but I still always managed to get a good night's sleep to get up for work.

I knew such "nightmares" would not cease to exist when I went to sleep at the army barracks, several states away. I would have my past that shaped me.

As I sat in the breakroom, I thought about my money situation. I knew I could be making more. And yet my mother said I should be glad to have a job.

Truly, though, I would have been crushed if Buck had not hired me soon after I was old enough to work in the 11th grade. I pulled out my wallet and looked at how much money I had: a five-dollar bill and two quarters. Not much indeed, but it was enough for lunch which, anyway, I always skipped until I was off work and would go home right next door to eat.

There would be no goodbye party for me. I would instead leave half sentimental, knowing Jamie would soon take my bagging position and subsequently move up, which was something I so didn't want to see happen, though I wouldn't be in town to see it anyway. So why did I care?

The time suddenly started going by quick instead of slow which, of course, was good. It meant I was enjoying life. I went through the victories and defeats, highs and lows of life as best I could, trying to see the downs and low points as things to learn from. I would not realize until later, after I had left, that how I felt on the inside was only partly predicted by where I was on the outside. It was up to me to be happy no matter where I was. It was all up to the individual.

Would I have to have to learn to be alone? Did I want that, if only because it meant little if any disappointments with people?

Maybe – if Darlene, in fact, never did fall in love with me and marry me – I would, when I least expected it, find another nice girl, though I knew I would never have the satisfaction from a female that Darlene's presence gave me.

I couldn't help but fantasize about living with her in her house, and the house was rent-free because it had been paid off. It would be so nice not to have to worry about money.

And then there was what would actually be. Indeed it would take winning the lottery for Darlene to marry me, and even then we may not be happy. It would be a marriage of financial convenience, indeed, for her, and it hurt me to realize that Darlene would only marry me for the millions I had won. But it was the only way such a dream of mine would come true.

Would I get tired of waking up in the morning with her in bed next to me? Indeed you could get sick of anything. I would want to believe that neither of us saw anyone or anything else but each other all the time, another fantasy. In truth, it would be the same situation of me not having any friends, except for people Darlene socialized with who only talked to me because I was married to her, along with those asking me for my lotto money.

And so there was the way I would want it and the way it would turn out. I would have to settle for the second of those after a lifetime of dreaming about the first that would, again, not occur, but it kept me going through bouts of depression and always had and always would.

In the vows of marriage, she and I would both vow to have and to hold each other, but I wondered if I would not know how to hold a woman in my arms as the only time I had ever done it was at the prom, dancing with Penelope, and everyone stared. Also, there was whenever I hugged my mother, but that didn't count. And so the romance life would indeed be new, uncharted territory for me, James Woods, who always looked at yearbooks on weekend nights to substitute for entertainment; for a social life.

I knew Buck would be really surprised when I came to visit during my breaks from the army. He, I knew, was planning never to see me again. Such was vital to his scheme. But before long I would be here again, defending my mother as much as I could from Buck, her new husband. And I knew he would not be able to stand it.

I figured Buck would probably make me feel quite unwelcome in that very house I was already rather disowned from anyway, and because by then my former bedroom would have no room because it would be filled with soup cans and chocolate, my "guest room" being, again, the grocery basement storeroom - with a mattress and a pillow - soon to be my new home anyway, if only for a few days. I knew thats how Buck would plot it.

But I would endure, and I would try to have an enjoyable time anyway during my breaks coming home from soldierhood.

And Buck would lie. That, too, I could easily predict. He would continue to talk about the soldier he never was, and the war medals he never actually got. And he knew I would be scared to death to ask to see those medals of honor because Buck knew he had everyone he knew well wrapped around his finger with fear, if only because he merely had that controlling personality.

And so it would go on: Buck would maintain and increase his vast grocery empire which – though in a way was nothing – meant something equally to him and I. It was the politics and money of both our lives.

18

The next morning seemed brighter as I was punching in at work even though Buck was looking at me like I was strange, meaning he was in one of his moods.

And yet I knew it was more than just a bad mood of his: it was an omen of what was to come. Something awful was going to happen because Buck had a mean streak; because he wanted something of my mother's. And I tried to be tough.

But I couldn't help but feel awful as I stood there at the timeclock looking at him. Buck, like my mother, was always the same: mood swings. And never, it seemed, anything else but that.

Buck had been part of my earliest memories. He was a very private person. His wife had left him, which was not surprising as Buck was not always the easiest person to get along with. He always seemed to like and get along with people I instead did not like or get along with, like Jamie.

Indeed it seemed that everyone that loved Missouri hated me, a sure sign that I did not belong in that state. Still, to me, it was home sweet home.

At the grocery that day, Buck was his usual unhappy self. Insecure, he would miss me to pick on.

Flipside to that too, though: Like Dale, Buck had been someone to talk to over the years, and at least when he was in a good mood, treated me like the son he never had – he again divorced, no children – but still I did not like how he took out his frustrations on me whenever he felt like it.

From what I knew about Buck's father, he would never have allowed Buck to treat me as he did. I had heard that Grandpa Buck Mellon always treated everyone who worked for him like they were a second family.

But Buck did not do that. Such level of kindness was not exerted by him, at least when he was in a bad mood, which was just about half the time.

And he could manipulate. Even then, with me having already signed the army contract so I now had no choice but to go anyway, Buck still stressed to my mother when she came into shop how I would "make a fine soldier." It was sad. And sick.

Buck handed me an orange.

"You know how to bag this, James. You've been doing it long enough." Was that an insult or compliment?

Buck confused me.

I heard Darlene mumble to a customer:

"Everyone picks on that kid" she said, hoping I did not hear it.

But I did, and I was sensitive. Then there wasn't time to get my feelings hurt anyway as the grocery filled with tourists.

Darlene looked at me, seeming to say "fragile."

I felt an adrenaline rush that she had noticed me. I smiled at her. She half-smiled back, busily doing the register.

A tourist fella standing next to me – who seemed to think of me as "his son" – whispered in my ear: "maybe you'll go dancing tonight son."

That made me smile. There were still some warm people in the world.

Hours later, I was still standing there bagging, glad to be having something to do as nightfall beckoned. I looked through the glass of the front of the grocery at the pebbles that led up to where they stared up at my bedroom window.

I could see the old bicycle that I hadn't ridden in years rusting against the wall of the house at which the pebbles ended. I felt it was a total mistake that I had spent any time getting that bike to work, as it was that badly rusted.

Darlene assisted in the bagging, her presence cheering me up.

"It will get better," she said.

She managed to get a smile on my face that day. Darlene always could. She was so wonderful that she would look back sometimes to see that I was still smiling. I loved her honesty and grace. It wasn't going to be such a bad day after all.

"My boy," she said.

Then Darlene realized that comment embarrassed me and she saw, perhaps for the first time, that I needed someone like her, albeit a girlfriend.

"Have you been dating?," she asked, still not having any sexual attraction to me, just being curious and, well, rather pitying me.

I blushed but loved the attention.

Darlene said "They don't talk to you at home, do they?"

"They do" I said, wondering how true that was.

"I just wanted to make sure you were all right," she said,

"And are you?"

I hated that people always said that to me. Darlene, like everyone, noticed my frown and always had to ask that question.

"I'm fine," I said.

Trying to change the subject, I said:

"Would you like some peanut butter to take home? We have tons of it at the house."

"No thank you," she said, "I'm not much of a peanut butter lover."

I would have logically stopped there if the stuff was not now piling up in my room.

"You have the right to feel that way, Darlene. You could give it to the homeless, though. My mom never wants to. She's that addicted to it."

"Thanks, James. You've got me thinking."

I knew that meant she didn't want it.

I saw with relief that Buck was now in the office, a place he usually stayed in a long time once he entered it. I wondered if Buck was still busy plotting whatever he was planning.

I looked around. Tourists running all over, excitement showing in their faces, their tour bus waiting outside that would wait as long as needed just to make money.

I had rarely seen anyone but them come in here. I had probably seen every breed of tourist – rich, poor, royalty, near homeless. All into one social class on the way to that arch that to me, again, was so dull. The only use it would have for me would be to break off a piece for a good luck charm: a charm I could use to win people's respect. Because I just never, ever got any.

19

My day off. I was lying on my bed after one of the final peanut butter eating encounters with my mother before I left Saturday, while also dealing with her ranting and raving about her unfair life. The quiet seemed strange after all that had happened that morning. It was already noon. Where did the time go?

I knew, much as I hated my job, that it was better to be working than not to be. Indeed my job had gotten me through the stress of things; it was an outlet my last two years of high school when I worked part-time at the grocery, and now full-time.

I knew my mother wanted me to be like Penelope: two grades behind me and studious – with Straight A's – she was a far cry from me who had never studied, I always having had taken general classes while she took advanced ones.

But I couldn't be something I was not. I was just James, and if people didn't like me for such, too bad.

I looked at myself in the mirror. Was I happy with me? I knew I was not. I always felt like I could do better, perhaps partly because people expected more from a male. But I knew that I didn't want to stand out. I didn't like that I was different and alone.

6pm. I walk down our stairs. I see Penelope go out the door, wondering why she comes in without knocking, leaves without saying goodbye to me. Into the kitchen to get another glass of fruit juice. I finish it and go into the living room. Mom is scarfing down peanut butter; it a sad look.

Still, I have to be proud of her for working so hard at something. She somehow gets over the fact that, like me, she doesn't have any friends. She looks chubby, despite being in her best clothes. At least she has fun with herself. She can forget about her problems a bit as she gobbles that stuff. She smiled big, all her teeth showing. Maybe she wants attention.

Mom took a break from eating, wondering what happened with Penelope.

"Did she get her feelings hurt again James?" said Ann.

'She gets her feelings hurt over anything," I said. "You have to give her attention all the time."

"She's been a good little friend to you, James."

I knew my mother did not know if that was true. After all, I was hearing that coming from a woman who essentially had friends that were peanut butter jars.

I wasn't sure about my mother or Penelope. I felt sort of embarrassed to be seen with either of them, and yet I knew that was how people might feel about me.

I said "Mom, do you get entertained with yourself?"

She looked at me and laughed.

I followed mom into the kitchen.

On the way in, I said:

"Are you feeling well?"

"Fine, but I was dizzy for a moment."

"Have you been eating peanut butter all day?"

Ann laughed. "Well, yes."

I hadn't had to ask that. I knew the answer. My mother was predictable.

"Maybe you feel dizzy because of all that you're eating. Take my advice: if you eat better, you'll feel better."

"But I've been in this routine so long," she said.

Ann sat out the next peanut butter eating session talking to me at the kitchen table. For the first time, my mother and I had a real, long conversation, something that had never really happened with mom always sheltering me, as mothers did.

"What kind of wife do you want, James?" she asked inquisitively.

She had no idea how much I loved Darlene. She just always figured it was puppy love. Something that would pass.

Ann said "I remember when you first started to do things with Penelope. I pushed you to go places her, but I had no idea you had no interest in who I thought would be just the right friend for you. I guess I was wrong. Sorry, James. I know you need more than your cousin."

"Mom, don't be so hard on yourself."

"I'm not much of a mom, actually" said Ann, putting her head down in shame.

"Not true mom. You've always tried to give a part of yourself to me."

My mother gulped down a final spoonful of peanut butter for the day as we sat there, as if it was a silent cry for help; to want to be noticed, as though a child nearing 52 years old.

Ann wasn't easy to live with, being neurotic and manic depressant seeming and all, but I knew I didn't have room to talk. She had long cleaned up the messes I left in both the kitchen and my bedroom, if only because she loved me.

Yet I couldn't help but ask myself, how did people manage to deal with such intense people as mom and I and how did two people so very intense – almost to the point of crazy – live with each other and not tear each other apart? After all, we were so much alike we often clashed. We were both heavy dreamers, and we both couldn't wait for something. In short, very obsessive.

My mother stopped eating and looked at me. "Are you working in the morning?"

Such was a stupid question as she had ironed my work clothes, but I didn't want to be rude to her, especially since things were about to get much worse between us.

"Yes, at 7am sharp."

I sensed my mother was a bit jealous that I had a job and she didn't. I was used to that as to her. She didn't know how good she had it.

Like with Buck and Darlene and Dale, sometimes it seemed like things were going to change for my mom. At some points, over the years, I thought she might out-grow the peanut butter thing and make friends and have a social life and all. But just like with the others in my life, it was to no avail. She was the same year after year: always having a one-track mind, always talking about the same things.

And such would follow a pattern. The beginning of which would, of course, be what seemed like the millionth time my mother said she was turning over a new leaf. And we would both look at each other excited. This was going to be it. The loneliness of the house was going to change. People were going to visit because my mother was going to make friends.

My mother would then go to social things: church bible studies, volunteering at the hospital on the other side of town. But always people didn't understand her, as was so with me. She – like I – stood out too much because her voice sounded funny. And so at the bible study, she would feel unwelcome, and the hospital would tell her they didn't need volunteers for a while as a way of lying so they wouldn't hurt her feelings.

Over the years, she would do the bible study and volunteer at the hospital things again and again, always to no avail. Always they seemed to dissolve because she was a little eccentric. Indeed I wondered if she – just as much as I – kept hanging around that town just to see what happened next.

And then my mother began to obsess.

"Why can't I be like other people?" she said out loud almost to the point that those at the grocery could hear it.

She was saying what I often felt, but never told anyone. It was as if I was looking at a mirror image of my inner thoughts as I stood there listening to her whine, which she did a lot of.

"You're too hard on yourself" I again said, trying to calm her.

And indeed, we were both too hard on ourselves. Both of us were obsessive perfectionists always, again, seeming to play a game with ourselves we were never able to win.

I patiently listened, trying to tolerate this person who was hard to live with. I knew I could run up the stairs or run out the door to get away from my mother and her problems, but that would just be running away, almost like running from the army without permission.

Indeed running from my mother at that point would sort of end up as a socially-dishonorable discharge as we all had to learn to deal with people related to us or not. It was life, and so I continued to sit there and listen to and love my mother.

An essentially dark cloud seemed almost to be hovering over our house then. And I tried to see the light in it, dealing with the ups and downs of life on that lonely road in that house with my mother.

I comforted her as much as I could with positive words but didn't know what to say after a while. In a way, my mother was a lost cause: past the point in life where you would have changed. For I had once heard that after a certain age level in life you probably were not going to change, and I feared I might end up like my mother when I was at the age she was at then.

And so there we both were, so much alike: lonely; terrible with people; different. Never had we had anyone but each other. And so I didn't see how I could up and leave her soon. Yet I was going to go crazy if I did not do so; if I did not move on from there. My mother turned her head away, feeling – I knew – that she just must be a drag to be around. And I didn't want her to feel that way. And so I tried to use humor and laughed. And then she did.

And then for a moment, at least, we both laughed up a storm as two crazy people would. And it was so good for both of us. And it felt as if we were the only two people in the world at all and were laughing about our eccentric selves.

It was weird, like the rest of the world was standing still as we sat there.

And so things had always waxed and waned that way in that house with its good and bad times. And soon I would be gone, and not long after – as time went by so fast – my mother wouldn't be around anymore at all.

20

Mom and I got into a deeper conversation about Penelope and my other friends or, better said, acquaintances. We talked about when Penelope and I, along with some others our age, went to see a play, which was supposed to be funny but was instead quite vulgar, in fact having a small bit of nudity and Penelope threw up.

"Everyone said they were never going anywhere with Penelope again, and Penelope said she had a weak stomach, but they all said that was no excuse to do it in the middle of a play, especially considering all the people who had paid good money to get in. They left Penelope and I standing there and took the bus back from St. Louis. One of the friends –a boy – was destined to be student council president his senior year of high school, but I found him hard to like, and it seemed that really he had nothing but frolickers and they all just wanted to get drunk" I told her.

While I wasn't a partier - no drinking and pre-martial sex - my mother never knew about me sometimes smoking cigarettes with Dale.

"At least Penelope liked me," I said, "and had the same values. But still, I wanted to be more with them so I could be popular,"

Ann was listening with a passionate face as I continued:

"It was Penelope's mother that came and got us because our "friends", if you could call them that, probably purposely forgot to give us our bus passes to get all the more away from Penelope and I."

"I got sick and they left us" Penelope said later to her mother, who came and got us, Penelope sniffling. Everything went wrong. We didn't even make it to the intermission with refreshments, which we were hungry for and thus so looking forward to,"

I asked my mother, "Why was it that everything I went through had to do with food?"

"Penelope's mother realized how upset Penelope was.

"Let's go home," she said.

"I have to fix your father's dinner."

"Penelope and her mother went into the bathroom to freshen up before the three of us left. Penelope's mother said to me as they came out, "Did you have a lovely day otherwise?"

"Yes, we did," I said, which was only half true. The others, not surprisingly, had shied away from Penelope and I the whole time.

"The nerve of those friends to leave you two there. They weren't worth knowing anyway," said my mother.

"Their lives are a popularity contest. When they get to college, they will be plain again" said Ann.

I was having so much fun conversing with my mother, it was like in an amusement park: away from my problems, experiencing the ultimate escape from life's stresses. And, too, I wished that both our lives could always be as such: that mom and I had been born perfect creatures who never had their bad, grumpy days along with our good ones.

My mother was so fun when she wanted to be. And she said the same about me:

"James, I wish you could always be like you are right now. You can be the sweetest, most fun thing when you want to be."

And I knew that meant I, like everyone else who was only human, had my downside: I could be very hard to get along with when I felt like it. I was far from the perfect child or perfect at always acting like a grown man.

But if you had no one else you had your family, and that was what I had.

Such was the reason, I knew, I had passed Senior English even though I hadn't studied for it or any other class I had in school. My teachers were all somehow related to mom and I, and so I rarely ever got a failing grade. A day in the life of America, that.

But my mother and I, much as we were blood to the town of Fell, were always very much shunned by it. We both stuck out like a sore thumb, neither of us ever having a real social life. And so my mother gobbled down peanut butter to get ready for the yearly contest and I looked at school yearbooks in my room on weekend nights. It was a dead end socially for both of us there.

"It's a miracle you made through high school, James" my mother said.

"I know, especially considering all those who drop out" I said.

We looked at each other in agreement.

"Don't feel bad if you never really had any friends in high school. I didn't. A lot of people don't. More than you think, in fact," she said, trying to comfort me in the loneliness she and I were always facing from people.

There we were, two Fell natives, glad to at least have each other in a town that pushed us out just as much as they were very much related to us.

"At least you have Penelope," my mother said with half a smile.

I knew mom wanted me, as her child, to be happy and to feel I had the whole world in my hands, which she knew I indeed did not. She knew that life in town had been like it was for her: far from easy, far from being accepted by anyone.

And I wanted to tell her about Dale. But she was already going to get so mad in a matter of hours that I didn't need any additional trouble between her and I.

"Penelope was at least someone to go the movies with growing up" she said.

"Yes, true mom" I said, deep down still wanting more in relationships.

The subject got back to the play:

"Wow James," my mother said about it, "it was like for once you had some normal friends and Penelope ruined it for you."

We looked at each other again, silently agreeing.

Us two conversing continued, it intimate, being there with who I had so much love, yet unfortunately at the same time knew was soon to disown me. Still, she would never in her heart stop loving me. How easy it was at this point to get along with people - blood or not - who in a few days I may never see again, like with people at summer camp.

"Penelope was in the car already. As we drove away from the big city excitement of the theatre, I remembered that Penelope had always been like this, and figured she didn't have to be. She could be socially adept. She didn't have to do things like throw up.

I sat in the back seat as the two of them sat in front and conversed, I wanting to open the handle of the door and fall out and end it all. I looked at Penelope and her mother. They seemed happy with whatever, just living every day. But I wanted more, always feeling excluded from the normal world that certainly wasn't them,"

I continued:

"As the car stopped at a light, I saw something odd: on a tree, there was something scratched about someone loving someone."

"That's right" said Penelope's mother when I mentioned it.

"Doesn't it interest you?," I said to both of them.

"I mean, do you ever try to figure out the definition of love?"

"We just want to go home and go to sleep" said Penelope, her mother agreeing and the both of them laughing.

"I felt so isolated. There were the two of them – nerdy, happy go lucky mother and daughter – and I was this poor guy in the back seat having to listen to them. I could not tell who on the inside was an adult and who was a child. Were they both children? Did Penelope's mother never really grow and stay on Penelopes level? It was sad how neither of them looked to have ever really grown" I said, depressed.

"Penelopes mother said "Why do people deface trees? I mean, they are living things."

"But, but… that wasn't my point," I said. "Two people loving each other were trying to tell other people about it; people who knew not who they were and were driving. Doesn't that move you?"

"What moves me is this car on this bumpy road" laughed Penelope's mother.

I gave up.

"I guess some people will do anything for attention" said Penelope.

"How awful," said her mother. "We as a society should get help for people like that."

"We?," I thought to myself. "The word is YOU. YOU need help. You both live like nuns."

"Put them in a support group with others who are the same," said her mother.

"Maybe start the American Society of Tree Abusers."

"I shrugged. There was no hope. I would always be alone or stuck with people like them for friends."

"There could be thousands like them, not just those two," said Penelopes mother.

"Can't the government, with all the money they have, give money for research into that kind of thing? They could call it Tree-itis. I mean, after all it first has to be given a name."

"The conversation was getting weird. Penelope and her mother WERE weird, and I wanted out of that car."

"Perhaps you two should take the initiative" I said to them sarcastically.

"Her mother, who had a mental maturity only because at her age one got it whether one liked it or not, was able to ignore my sarcasm as only someone's mother could do:

"But it shouldn't just be the strong taking care of the weak. It has to be getting them to help themselves,"

Penelope's father was a high school guidance counselor, and so I figured her mother had heard her husband say that.

"They, the government, already take care of rather a lot of people. All the welfare families they pay. All the people of this country – the taxpayers – they serve. And so they could give more for the disturbed. But still, you have to want to change" continued Penelopes mother.

"There's also the question of, should there be a fine for writing on a tree? I mean, isn't that like littering?" said Penelope.

"By now I was almost asleep. I was so bored. These two people were confused and disorganized. They were not part of society. I was not learning anything from them."

Indeed I never learned anything from that town. Everyone was the same. So much in fact that it was almost scary. I had about never met anyone intellectual, save for the highly educated tourists that sometimes came through my line and said they graduated from Harvard or Yale, and even then they could have been lying.

"I couldn't wait for that car ride to be over" I said to my mother as our conversation that evening neared an end.

"I would feel that way too" my mother said with concern.

"I almost felt they were making fun of me."

"Are you ok back there, James?" Penelopes mother said to me, laughing.

"I was embarrassed as the car turned into my driveway. The car stopped at the tip of the garage door, almost hitting it because Penelope's mother couldn't drive. We saw you, mom, stick your head out the door and wave, not wanting to be seen in the nightgown you were still wearing. I ran up to the door. The car pulled away.

"Just a minute" you yelled, trying to stop the car because you wanted to tell Penelope's mother something.

We stared at you in surprise as you ran. Two months ago you had seemed much thinner than you did presently, even though you have always been chubby.

"Ann, what happened to your weight?" Penelope's mom said.

You didn't know what to say. But I knew the situation: That soon to happen contest meant a lot to you, and to win it you had to practice eating a heck of a lot of peanut butter and thus gain a heck of a lot of weight."

My mother and I smiled at each other in understanding. We would miss being away from each other, but it was time I saw new places and faces. The end of childhood and innocence had come.

21

I awoke, wishing I was in a dream, it seeming just like any day. But no. Dream it was not and worse day of my life it was to be. Tonight, Buck was to come. He'd knock, and even with the years I spent mentally preparing for it, I wasn't ready.

Later, down in the kitchen, I ate breakfast hastily, having a hard time concentrating on the two things that dominated me – food and fate – at once. Together they were the story of my life, about to explode in a soap opera-like climax that I wished I could more fully predict, but Buck had too masterfully planned – always had – for me to know much about.

And it had always been that way too: I always in the dark concerning it. When I would try to get the truth out of Buck while we worked on car parts in the yard as I was growing up, he would be silent. And so, like the defendant in the courtroom never saying a word – just letting his lawyer do all the talking – Buck thought so much of himself that he seemed to believe he had the right to remain silent whenever he felt like it.

And what about my rights? My feelings?: What would they be after the fact? Would there be closure after I was disowned, or just the beginning of the saga? Had Buck Mellon barely scratched the surface when it came to destroying me? I wondered.

Food would always be what the gears turning in Buck's head were made of. He knew the way to anyone heart – their gullibility – was through their hunger. Hunger and smelling things good to eat. That was that man's ploy. Just like Adolf Hitler once said, "if you want to control their minds, control their music."

I knew how very wrong it was to compare Buck to someone who had killed six million people. Buck was nowhere near that kind of person, still I couldn't help feel deep down that he was a grocery dictator that affected every second of my life.

I was a weakling, a laugh of a boy who was just too kind, feeling I needed to bring Dale his daily secret meal. But Dale had been male bonding for me, just like Buck, who I had been able to talk to about stuff.

And yet Buck and Dale only ever gave me attention, showed interest in me to get something, and I didn't want to accept something that had been going on much too long, namely letting those two take advantage of me.

Too late to change now anyway. And yet I didn't want it to change. Change was harder for me than anything else. It meant pain. There wasn't any pain in staying in or going back to the situation you were in.

I stood up from the table, trying to feel as if the whole world were listening and yelled out:

"BUT JAMES, THE MAN, YOU'RE SOON BRAVING A NEW SITUATION."

And I held my glass of chocolate milk up, pretending to do cheers with it with someone else, trying not to feel alone in the positive search for me.

Then no more cheers with the invisible. I sit down again in my kitchen chair, wanting to be friends with the jar of jelly at almost nineteen. Jars, park benches, payphones. All of these things I had grown attached to in a really weird way because I wanted companionship, and so I fantasized about having such with inanimate objects.

I looked back on the days gone by — days when I was a kid who had names for my shoes — and I had a wet dream in the eighth grade. And the ultimate event in my childhood: the prom with my freckle-faced cousin Penelope in my senior year and everyone stared.

And graduation. And waking up the day after that, and then driving by my high school a year later. Such a bittersweet feeling for everyone that goes through that.

I thought about Penelope. In a few days her senior year of high school would start, and as she had always been determined to get it, Penelope would be yearbook editor, big stuff – indeed quite political – in this small hammock called Fell, Missouri. Every year, being head of the yearbook in the town's only high school was a big deal, and everyone talked about what the book was going to have or shouldn't be lacking in.

But some people just had to have attention, though no one was better at covering up their insecurities than Penelope, who endured many a joke – many an insult – because she was fat, which only drove her further to achieve. To have a 4.0 average. Whatever it took to show everyone what she could do.

I, on the other hand, was in no way a big high school achiever. I wished I could be like Penelope. I wished I could be like a lot of people. But I could only be me, a loner who just pretended to do cheers with someone and poked at his scrambled eggs.

22

The day at work - the same day of "the night event"- came quick.

I raced out the door. Just twenty seconds before timeclock tardiness and I barely made it, just like when I would race to catch the school bus, too seeming pointless, because what was the gain in the long run, really?

It seemed like every day as the week went on, I had to try harder to get to work on time, as I was a little more tired all of the six days I worked until my day off. It was rather a little ritual of fighting wanting to sleep with getting up for the sake of just trying to live my life, as far as I was concerned.

Sometimes I wondered why I bothered with all I did. Indeed sometimes, at work, I again wanted to throw my hands up in the air and walk out. But my mother and Dale and Penelope had all said to be sure and not do that. And they helped me to realize that, indeed, you didn't know what you had until it was gone.

And I would surely miss the job if I let it slip out of my hands by quitting without notice, though it would be a delight to Buck, who had thought that I would in fact have given in to his abuse by then and just quit.

I bagged, trying to show half a smile. I thought of what mom might be making me for lunch, then remembered she was gone and someone else would be home with me that night. A visitor, almost like facing an enemy soldier on the battlefield, it was so filled with mistrust between them and I.

American flags hung all around. The grocery walls brimming with red, white, and blue. Buck missed no beat: he was going to remind me of the importance of patriotism – of soldierhood – to the very end. I sadly stood there looking at the stars and stripes used to manipulate me. What kind of country was America coming to, its very flag abused towards a U.S. citizen?

I could only throw myself into my work: bagging, hoping it would take away some of the pain. It helped, at least some. Still, I had fear of the unknown; of things to come.

I had to smile on the job, working hard to do so, if only for the customers who didn't want to see employees frowning.

From down in the storeroom, I carried up soup cans in my arms to put them with others already stacked. Loved my work.

23

I stood near the front door, it six in the eve. He coming knocking, it almost pre-destined. I knew everything that could go wrong was going to. Buck would sink my ship of hope for self-esteem, at least for a long time. It was a very real challenge. I tried to mentally reassure myself that things would work out somehow, as my mother said my late father used to always say. But somehow, I could not help but feel that the night was nothing but doom for me.

"Why was I the only one these things happened to?" I couldn't help but ask myself, and I had been asking myself that as to many things in my life for a while.

I fantasized that my dreams had come true: marrying Darlene, me owning the grocery and telling Jamie what to do instead of it being the other the way around, which I knew it would be if I came back from the army and tried to work at the grocery again.

I looked around the house. My mother never changed or moved furniture. Always there were open and empty peanut butter jars everywhere, as my mother was, again, just like me as far as being messy.

Despite mom's same ways, she wanted me moving on; growing. Still, she sheltered me. Talked me out of things: being a substitute teacher because "the kids were vicious" and "if something happens to one of those kids, you'll go to jail."

I knew she was right, so I never worked for the school system at all, in any capacity. Mom was that powerful an influence. She could talk me into or out of anything. Sometimes I did wonder if she knew anything at all, in a generation far removed from mine.

When I was upset, my mother knew it.

"What's wrong?" she'd say when I came home from work, someone - usually Buck - having hurt my feelings.

"Nothing," I'd say, not wanting to knock the job. Waited a lifetime for the thing.

She'd be silent, not liking a confrontation, but not go stand up to Buck either they, again, friends since childhood.

"I'm just really tired" I'd always say.

And that would be the end of it, and I would watch TV, go to sleep depressed, and the next day climb out of bed again for another day at work; another round of both fighting and laughing about things with Buck, his personality going back and forth between nice and mean. A roller coaster of emotions.

I continued daydreaming about my mother, about times she tried to encourage me:

"You should be proud of what you're doing, working hard. A lot of people your age aren't doing anything but just loafing, just not doing anything but going to the mall up the way."

She was right, but it didn't help. For still I had difficulty dealing with people, no matter how comforting my mother's words were.

"You're right mom; I do work hard. And you work hard to be a great mother."

And when I said that it was like my mother lit up, as if no one ever said anything good about her to herself either. And I realized my mother often had a hard time with people too; she just had a mental maturity to blow it off easier than me.

And for once, I saw that my mother was anything but dumb. She had lived through many Missouri economic depressions - pre-arch days - and had dealt with the death of her late husband, my of course late father that I had never gotten to know as he was, again, killed while away in battle when I was three.

End of daydreaming. I looked at the clock. It was now fifteen minutes after six. I knew Buck's timing. He always left work right about now. I had to hang in there with all my might and be polite when I answered the door and it was him.

And I knew I would not want to answer it. I would instead want to leave Buck waiting at the door until he gave up and left, but I absolutely could not do that, as he would know what I was doing, and had the nerve and the will to wait there at the door forever anyway, because when Buck wanted to be rude, he really could be. And so he would invite himself on me.

Time slowed down. Not a good sign, as it meant I was not enjoying life, enjoying the moment. Indeed I was being used like never before by only one possible person in the world, and I had no control.

There I was, like in a kind of time warp, between a dull past and, in a few moments, my life about to change forever. What would I say to Buck when I answered the door? It would be hard to be hospitable, I bitter already and he hadn't even pulled the stunt yet, my mother soon to turn against me, yet we would always love each other, even with Buck in the way as my stepfather pulling against me as much as he could, at least when in a bad mood.

24

Three knocks.

I didn't want to answer the door, as if the Devil had come knocking. And why? Almost as if I had sold my soul? Given up my ticket to heaven to have the stamina to hang in there against Buck? But I had to answer it. I couldn't leave him out there waiting.

It would be hard when he came in. I would have to make him feel welcome, as with any visitor in one's home, while it was at the same time anything but just a visit, but instead the culmination of almost 19 years of planning and waiting to destroy me.

Yes, I had to answer it. Yes, Buck wasn't going to leave, persistent fellow. Buck would win whatever he plotted for that night, really only my residence until the middle of the night – when mom got home from the contest then – and I disowned. And indeed, in a way, I again didn't live there already, so I might as well answer the door and let Buck stay. Then go live somewhere else. That was what was going to happen anyway.

He came in with a barbeque grill, I not sure just how that was one of his scheme tools.

"I thought I'd show you how to cook burgers on the grill outside, in case you didn't know," he said with a smirk.

I felt like he was insulting me.

Right into the backyard he went, setting up the grill and soon cooking those burgers. Why did they smell so strangely good, that part of the appeal of his manipulation? The finest beef just like he paid to have the finest chocolate in the grocery to woo my mother? Again, me and food. He had known me long enough to know I got hungry about now: 6:30 in the eve.

As he flipped the patties, he sang. And it was hard to resist what he was offering because I was hungry and wasn't a good cook.

Buck was singing " America the Beautiful" loud enough for me and our scant few neighbors to hear it.

As he was again humming the words "Oh Beautiful, for Spacious Skies" almost to be screaming, he poured gasoline all over me, and I looked at him in amazement.

"Take a joke," Buck said, "it's just like a college prank when you are in the shower, and someone comes in and throws a bucket of cold water on you."

And I believed him. I trusted him, or at least wanted to; wanted to have a friend to believe in me. "Okay," Buck then said, "the jokes over. Go up and take a shower to wash it off."

25

I started to walk up the stairs to the bathroom ever so slowly. I didn't like another man telling me what to do, much less when to bathe. And I knew it was somehow part of the trap. Buck was going to pull something while I was taking a shower, something that would have been in the planning for almost two decades, or in easier terms, as long as I had been alive. Whatever was going to happen, I always knew, was going to have to do with food. I did not know, though, it would also involve fire and water.

But I knew I smelled something as I was about to turn on the shower. Something was amiss downstairs, all right. And then I saw it: Smoke was seeping under the door. BUCK HAD LET THE FIRE GET ALMOST TO THE BATHROOM BEFORE I COULD WASH OFF THE GASOLINE SO HE COULD PULL SOMETHING!

And I remembered those chocolate chip cookies that Buck had told me to put in the oven to cook. THEY WOULD HAVE BEEN MADE WITH MOM'S

FAVORITE EUROPEAN CHOCOLATE! He had let the cookies not just burn, but catch fire and almost destroy the house. And Buck knew my mother would never forgive me if I did something as irresponsible as accidentally start a fire stemming from her favorite chocolate!!!

And if I cried, it would not change a thing. It was just life, as real as the fact that someone was going to be a dead soldier while someone else would get to live through it, almost like the luck of the draw. Like your name was picked out of a hat of pieces of paper with people's names on them. It might be you selected, or it might not be.

Why did it always seem to be me that got picked as people's scapegoat, though? That I would always wonder. That I had never been able to figure out for as long as I could remember.

For a few seconds I just stood there behind the shower curtain and let it be, which was what Buck wanted: for me to be helpless. Mom was going to be furious when she got home, and I had to be ready for it.

I coughed. More smoke had filled the bathroom than I thought as I threw open the shower curtain as a bare man wanting the company of a woman. I was so sexually frustrated and so alone in dealing with the intense smell of whatever was burning, which seemed like it was the whole world going into destruction at once.

At least that was how I saw my world at the moment: shriveling up like a newspaper thrown into a fire, no hope of any life, of any existence to be useful to anyone for any purpose.

Life passed before me. Time not to be crouching back behind the toilet. Does a real man just let it happen?

But what to do? How to run through the flames when covered with gasoline?

Whose fire was it? The fire Buck started, the fire of hell, or an earthly combination of both: of hell on earth, and I'm the only one on it? And so couldn't you go to hell early?

Quite early, if people gave you a hard time while trying to find who that was inside: personal angels or demons forming my character?

Then I saw it. I shuddered. There WAS the blasted thing. The rope I once swung on out my window pretending to be Tarzan. Buck had moved it to the bathroom window so If I used it to escape the fire I would look like a coward, just like a soldier afraid to die for his country. Who amongst your people would let you live that down?

Should I die? Is that what you should do when living becomes more of a risk? If I beat this situation, Buck would never talk to me again.

Cup my ear to the floor. There's rocking. Easy to imagine thoughtless Buck possibly even asleep as he rocked while the flames raged. Buck had that much nerve. Everything he did – even when asleep – had to do with his plan. Creak it did as I shrieked in terror, trying to be mature about it.

There was no choice but to swing on the rope out the window and down to safety, living with disownment, knowing I had done nothing to no one.

Buck knew the same, and he planned it all out so long ago. The peak of life's unfairness. To beat it was to lose. To expect icing on the cake was to be a fool.

I fantasized – me in an ideal world. The smoke and flames are becoming Darlene, standing on the ashes, proud of my courage. Buck, the one who lost, forever then on treating me with respect, looking forward to me coming back from the army to work at the grocery in management. How nice if you could wish stuff to be, wish stuff away. But instead the power of greed raged as much as the fire did.

Swing like Tarzan on the rope or burn to death. At least either way there would be victory: as no matter what I had so far taken chances – hung around to see what happened next. And so that I had tried hard at all – worked at my situation – had been a victory. And I could always hold on to the hope that maybe my story would inspire someone else. Be a challenge to others misunderstood because they looked young.

And yet there was the flip side, it seeming a no-win situation either way: for if I lived, I would have to face my mother never again claiming me, and if I died, everyone might think I did so because I felt I didn't have what it took to be a soldier. And I cared very much what they all thought. I wanted to believe I was "the man." But I was not going to be the renaissance man who could do anything staring back from the mirror and the flames, the two almost one and the same.

I started to climb out the window, the flames licking at me. I started to black out from the stress and the fumes, while at the same time hearing the sound of someone coming. Had Buck changed his mind and wanted to save me? Somehow I knew that was not the case, everything then going dark. The puzzle of my life broken up into complicated pieces, which could only be put together by myself. And that may take as long as figuring out the Rosetta Stone.

26

I didn't know how long I had been unconscious. I opened my eyes on another mattress but no different the insecure man I was in dealing with the things I saw.

I knew this grocery basement storeroom was going to be my new home, at least for a few days. They would be the most difficult days of my life, harder than anything the military –which I was soon to enter into - could dish out as far as pressure. The test of character Buck was laying down upon me was, to me, far more difficult than being tested on any physical battlefield with guns and enemies facing you.

Boxes of chocolate bars filled the basement storeroom - I for the millionth time comparing them to a tomb of unknown soldiers, waiting for me to be buried along with them. They didn't give off a certain sweet smell for nothing. Nestled between the chocolate boxes I saw a shotgun, which made me sink even deeper into depression. Seeing it made me realize that this indeed was my new home; that I was surely now to be a 3rd shift security guard for the grocery so that Buck could save on alarm fees from the police department.

I quickly realized that my life was about never to be the same: I was about to be un-fairly and un-justly cut out of my mothers will and be stuck here, living in the grocery almost as bad off as the homeless man in the woods I had secretly long brought food to. And there were the bars on the window. I did not know if they were to keep burglars out or to keep me in. While Buck couldn't physically hold me prisoner, I knew he could have installed those bars on the window solely for a feeling of power: for having total control of me as a grocery slave and future stepson fool.

I wished I could turn back time and go back to before Buck had set my house on fire and then go back even further to before I was born. That was how depressed I was. It was as if I was grieving because I had died inside. But I couldn't give up. I was determined to see everything as a cup half full, not half empty, discouraging as the circumstances were.

27

Unique - in my problems. Alone in a big wide world that seemed, indeed, to be made for the brave and to prey on the weak. The world was a stressful place.

And so the aroma of barbeque chicken – which in my moment of crisis had been replaced with the smell of smoke – was now for me the sweet smell of european chocolate, a perfect example of how pleasant and fake – to use as a play on clean and fake – went together.

The smell was the only thing nice about what I was experiencing. The other senses – namely seeing – were bleak in what they saw. The climax of almost two decades of manipulative planning by my boss at the grocery and soon to be stepfather – Buck Mellon – was now taking place, and to me it felt like the world was coming to an end, for I was going to have to face blame and disownment by my mother when she came and saw the damage to the house.

It was a sight for sore eyes as I looked around the storeroom: I hated these walls. And yet I loved them, if only because they were familiar. And so, too, how could I not both hate the chocolate because Buck had ordered it out of manipulation and yet love it because it was my mother's favorite, the two happenings not a coincidence but, again, rather a classic manipulation of Buck's?

And so all around me were both memories and circumstances together: the dwelling across the street that had been the only house I had ever known; the floor I lay on that I had walked on a thousand times unpacking boxes as an employee and now was the floor that was my new home, if only for a few days; the grocery storeroom door out to the job that loved me and yet soon to open to a mother that I loved but was about to disown me.

I was about to experience, when the storeroom door opened, my angry mother and my boss and future stepfather yelling at me in a sick game of Buck's manipulation.

And wasn't I, again, still going to feel the pain of it all even when I was many states away? Would it just feel like a time of standstill until I came back here again to live one day of which I would, too, for several reasons: familiarity, owning the grocery, and my life-long love cashier Darlene?

And then, laying there, I realized something terrifying: Buck had carried me here after I passed out in the bathroom covered with gasoline like he was carrying a dead soldier to burial. That was how he had planned it to seem: like I had died on the inside; died alive. I shuddered, smelling like gas, as I had not even turned the shower on when the fire came at me. Buck had timed it so I purposefully wouldnt be able to turn on the shower in time, and pass out from the flames covered in gasoline and he came and carried me away to safety just in time, ALL TO BE MANIPULATING! THAT SNAKE!

28

It was the dark of night as I sat on another bunch of steps: the grocery basement storerooms, only in a way the steps of home as these steps had never been - and would never really be - mine.

They were coming soon. But I tried to sit there fearless, which didn't work. Instead, I was scared of my own shadow as it counted down.

I knew by now that no one else in the world could compare themselves to what had always, strangely, been bad luck for me, food: the food here at the grocery; food to bring Dale; food that was peanut butter my mother gobbled down to practice for the next contest; and finally food at Buck's nice little bbq from which I almost burned to death earlier.

Though food situations had always followed me, and even though I knew it would be part of my boss's ultimate victory - at least if you considered our fight over my mothers will, which might as well be his, for it was going to be – I never thought Buck would risk my life as closely as he did with that "prank." He really must have seen me as shrinking while Buck became more and more of a giant who could eat whoever he wanted.

Then I do something immature. I lay on the top of the steps, face down, and slide down them as I did as a kid at home. My whole front body is, of course, brushed by the wood, and then I stop, bored. I am pondering again. Thinking that no one my age would do that. But at least no one would ever know I did it. I want to scream out to the darkness: WHY IS IT LIKE I AM INVISIBLE?

The confrontation with my mother and Buck is a squeak away. I must be ready. Tact, poise, even lying to save Buck's skin. I want this job that much. Life that unfair. But that man is going to win. However, I could win a small victory to know who was that staring back from the mirror? Why did I feel caught in my twisting, changing reflection that was a hallucination until I found me? Why did it seem like I would be the one that would crack mirror after mirror in heaven and be forgiven for it by God always, but eventually Buck would be up there seeming his usual self, yelling at me for it?

There I was, laying across the bottom of the steps, as if trapped and suspended in time and success, my adrenaline seeming to have frozen and then melted and then taken on a life of its own - as far as despair - in my love dreams and hopes; my business aspirations. I suddenly started to feel no drive for those things. Maybe I really had died inside? Perhaps this storeroom was essentially the burial place of my spirit?

And just like success and failure could be defined differently by how people looked at it, how did one define what adrenaline was supposed to be for? Was it for normal, conventional people who had luck getting dates? Should I, then, even have had it in the first place? It always gave me a high, but then I ended up all dressed up with nowhere to go. Thus my "friends" were yearbooks and the park bench I sat on and bugging the operator on the payphone next to it.

Why did it seem like only I had highs and lows? Why couldn't my brain be developed like everyone else's? What stunted it? Maybe too much McDonalds and other "junk food"? I didn't know. But I knew I deserved better than being in that storeroom in the middle of the night, unable to sleep because of what was happening and what was about to happen, though there were worse things than being disowned.

But it would pass, for everything did but God. Still, it would be a long time. Overtones that were sure to be almost permanent. Meaning more damage to my few relationships than I might think.

29

I laid on the mattress looking at the ceiling, seeing it as some mirror to heaven that could tell me my future. And while I did it, I didn't smell chocolate or ashes. I smelled – fully sensed – Male Menopause.

Such a thing shouldn't come until 50, but I was so eccentric that I was a child, teenager, adult, and older man all rolled into one. I struggled with constantly being one of the four every fifteen minutes.

The ceiling was barren, like my life, like the back wall of the grocery I had stared out to from my bedroom window all my life.

I wanted the ceiling to turn into clouds. Clouds that shaped into things of meaning. Into the shape of what I looked like when I was given the papers that said I officially owned the grocery. Into happy blue skies – representing how my life could have been so far – for always I had dreamed the impossible, hoping one day my ship would come in.

I laid there, naked as if dying on a cross, knowing I must get some clothes on if I was going to confront those two. But there was something beautiful above me laying there naked, wanting the ceiling to go from sky blue clouds to a beautiful image of Darlene's body. But instead it was the same old thing: Blah life. Yearbooks. Playing with payphones. No winning contest numbers. No romances.

I got up and put my clean clothes on, as Buck had put a basket of my clean clothes next to the mattress (he didn't miss a beat). But still I felt like a burned wreck.

Lying down looking at the ceiling again I was one of those imagined clouds, changing form to please people, which never happened, yet still the same insecure cloud James no matter how the cloud looked on the outside. I so much felt like a black cloud, never a blue one, wishing I could not be a cloud that was going to rain.

I essentially lived in a dungeon. A weird, dead chocolate soldier kind of dungeon about to be eaten and forgotten about along with them. But I was not a cloud, and I was not a chocolate bar. I was a real, living human being and I couldn't figure myself out, my image in mirrors hazy, not wanting to reveal the real me as if to symbolize life's unfairness.

It was as if I was lying there dead because, in a sense I had, once more, died inside. Died while still alive. No funeral, no victory medal for what I had survived. Indeed if funerals were for people who were not dead, just died inside, I wondered if anyone would come to that one of mine, either. Though in truth, my many relatives that made up the town would come, if only because it was appropriate. Otherwise, like Buck wanting something, they would about never give me the time of day.

I carried on my little nap on the old mattress, little things making me happy – as it went with men – and little things making me miserable because I was sensitive as I continued to look up at the ceiling, wishing answers would appear above me like a mirage out of the desert.

It wouldn't be long now. I had to mentally prepare for what was not going to be good. Again and again, I wished I could lay on things like that mattress forever, away from my problems, from what ailed me, fantasizing about having all the money, all the love in the world.

But defining love was as difficult as defining who I was. I wished there could be a mirror image of me - in human form standing next to me, just like a twin - to learn from. But then I would probably be scared of them. And so maybe I wanted my image in my "life mirror" to be blurry. Maybe I didn't want to see how I was.

I could sense it. I was about to hear the clickety-clack of my mother's shoes, and the clomp-clomp of Buck's work boots. It was as predictable as for those who felt the Titanic was going to sink. It wasn't unsinkable, but unsinkable were my hopes, my spirit: those things would give me life in my depressing insides if anything did.

As it counted down to less than a minute I stood up, looking around at my new home, my dungeon storeroom, at least having the glory of being porter, which was just a professional name for night watchman or security guard. But I accepted the position with excitement for the grocery was, again, as much my life as it was Buck's.

I now stood at the foot of the steps, imagining the climb up them to be never-ending, as if such a thing was something from hell. Indeed I didn't want to walk up to the last step, for it was easier to be a coward here at the beginning than to reach the last step, but I had to climb every rung of those old stairs to face an explosive climax.

Back and forth my life went - between being in hell and imagining life heavens – it almost dizzying, as if heaven and hell could both be experienced right here on earth, a thing that seemed made to happen to me.

Though I tried to deny it, I really did wish the devil was coming to open the storeroom door instead of my mother and Buck. The devil disowned everyone already. The devil was negative, just like me, so he would act less surprised about the situation. But, too, the devil could disguise himself as anyone or anything he wanted, even a grocery boss.

And so perhaps the range of my life relationships had been filled with devils in human form, giving only me a hard time.

They were outside, and it did feel like I had reached the end as I heard the rush of their clomping and clickety clack shoes come to a stop. My mother and Buck were talking to each other loudly, their voices carrying like mine always did, though never like theirs or anyone I knew.

"Your voice carries" people would always say to me, another reason to give me a hard time.

But nothing was going to equal this. I might as well go live on another planet after this confrontation. Something had now happened between mom and I, and Buck was going to love it.

I wished my biggest concern at present was to get up to the main grocery floor to start my grocery porter duties. I was a grocery night security guard now, whether liking it or not.

But no. Instead, there was the reality that in an instant, mom was going to disown me for the fire because she was just plain helpless to know anything but to obey Buck because being a woman and having a dependent personality and being ever lonely, she wanted to be controlled, even if only because it meant someone was interested in her.

I just wished she knew that the wedding ring Buck was going to present to her right after I left was really for his own selfish, business/real estate reasons, part of a long-running master plan that had been going on for as far back as I could remember.

I had too many of my own concerns to deal with to be able to help my mother or anyone else, constantly asking myself: Would my my dreams come true? Would I find romance and lots of money and even if I did, would I still be unhappy? Should I carry it on with the current situation in this town and never go somewhere else? Never take chances? The answer seemed to be no.

I was too smart to not get out there in the world and try. And yet I had so little confidence to do so, which I knew would show in the big wide real world as it had in my life so far. I wished I could fake it like other people, but my face was a dead giveaway to my insecurities. And I knew people noticed. I had hoped that by then things would be different; that I would have changed and grown and finally had a social life in that town. But I couldn't fool myself into thinking that was so when it was not.

Indeed, you always had problems – for me, loneliness – no matter what age you were. And that day – as an eighteen-year-old grown man who was now not a kid anymore - I felt quite alone in the world, even in such familiar surroundings as my hometown, with most of the town, again, related to me.

As I stood there in the grocery basement storeroom in the dark of night, I tried to fantasize as to what I was hearing: Oh, I just thought I heard something. Was someone trying to break in the grocery? It was my job to investigate, but really I only halfway cared - half business-minded, half bitter - for partially the grocery was my life and dream, and partially I hated it and the entire town outside it, blaming my problems on it all in a feeling of circumstances that could, again, have gone some other –better - way in my life so far. And then there wasn't a sound at all - a kind of dead silence – making me feel like I was in a sort of solitary confinement.

I fantasized further, imagining myself proceeding to go up into the main grocery to see if there was, in fact, a security problem. But for a moment - before I did that - I looked out through the bars on the storeroom window and up at the window that, until earlier, was where I had always peered out to the world just thinking in my lifelong bedroom.

And now here I stood looking out to that past, in this depressing basement storeroom, trying to be excited about the future that I knew may well not be any more exciting, just a different place.

I realized I might never get the chance to show my talents – business or otherwise – because of the selfish and pre-conceived notions of that town I hated, yet felt so close to as well. But why should I have felt close to people who thought I couldn't do anything right anyway? That I had always been wondering.

Again, it was just the comfort of the familiar; of familiar faces speaking in an ignorant tongue, but they were my people. They were my culture and roots and I would never feel as close to any people in the world ever again in my life. How nice – though I had always been around people who doubted my abilities – to have had something stable; the familiarity of the same things all my life.

Then I snapped out of my fantasies, hearing them again.

I turned around and looked up at the storeroom door. It was, of course, no burglar. I almost wished it was in that, like the devil, even a burglar almost seemed better.

A burglar could shoot me in cold blood, but I felt I was already – perhaps worse - for the millionth obsessive time, going to die inside in a minute anyway. It felt like a witch hunt. I didn't know how I was going to explain the damage to the house to my mother. And Buck's presence wouldn't be much help. Indeed Buck made it – let it – happen.

But I both really couldn't prove it and was afraid to say anything against Buck that would knock my job – one I had waited, again, all my life for.

I started to hear the doorknob rattle.

What would I say? Ann would surely be a changed person altogether, if only after years of being brainwashed by Buck to now, finally, being surely completely against me. There was no way to run out of the storeroom. All I could do was grit my teeth and hope for the best.

The doorknob started to turn.

Almost in an instant, I was going to face the wrath of my boss's plan that had been building up for years to this point. For a second, the knob went silent. I wondered if maybe Ann and Buck were admiring how nice the grocery looked, both of them partly not wanting to be hard on me, but neither of them ever changed: Buck was mean and Ann was a sucker and those things as to them, I knew, were for always; for all time, because people didn't change.

And neither did one's situation if one moved to another area, although I didn't want to face that reality any more than facing disownment by my mother.

I walked to the stairs and just sat there, thinking, why worry about what I had no control over anymore? If Ann was no longer going to claim me, then what could I do?

Then the doorknob started to turn again and I swallowed hard, having always feared the unknown, and yet I had long predicted what was about to happen anyway. An inevitable, new chapter was about to start in my life. They opened the basement door and I walked through, scared to death.

30

She was as silent as the moonlit quietness of the grocery, and I knew it meant she was mad. I could hardly stand it as I stood there, made worse with Buck just plainly standing there getting his way, having no compassion for me whatsoever, but instead just glad to know that he had accomplished his almost two decades old mission to turn Ann against me.

And yet, some of the pain was not there because I had, of course, always known that this "disownment" from my mother was coming. For I wasn't stupid: I could see the writing on the wall; the sinking ship that was my destiny as far as relationships in that town, even with my flesh and blood mother, who Buck now had complete control of, he almost waiting any second to slip a wedding ring on her finger.

And then the urge. The urge I felt just to let go and scream as loud as I could and beat Buck black and blue. But, being rational and law-abiding, I just stood there and held it all in: my frustration for all of life's unfairness; the half of me that hated Buck along with the other half of me that wanted to be just like him, at least business-wise.

And so for business reasons, I kept my cool. For maybe if I let Buck have his way fully, there might be the payoff one day of having the grocery. One never knew how things could go even if, also, a lot of things weren't likely.

I was essentially just an inanimate object – say, a food item at the grocery – who was helpless to fight. But all I could do from that point was what I had always done: hang on despite my lack of self-confidence. Always I held on to the hope that maybe one day, things might turn around. One never knew.

And I wished, immature as it was to feel so, that I did not have to wait any longer for things to get better. How nice, I thought to myself, if we could always have what we wanted right away. But that wasn't how it was going to work.

Instead, I would have to go someplace else and prove something, bringing back war medals – like a diploma – to show physical proof that I did achieve something despite all of the people in town who didn't think I could.

Neither my mother nor Buck said a word as they stared back, and back I went downstairs to try to sleep as they both left. I had been yelled at in the worst possible way: silent disownment.

31

Later, as I climbed the creaky steps up to the main floor of the grocery to do my porter duties, there was at least the comfortable feeling of the steps underneath me and the drab storeroom in which I now lived being familiar. I began to wonder if there was anyone who secretly did not fear the unknown?

The grocery looked and felt as cheerful as the neighboring funeral home which, in turn, made the chocolate boxes strewn around the grocery seem all the more like unknown soldiers in body bags, again waiting to be embalmed and, again, always it seemed like I was soon to join them as I was rather being pushed out of town for the army in a few days by Buck anyway, feeling as powerless as the chocolate.

It was as if the chocolate bars were laying in state, obeying Buck because they were rather unconscious; because they didn't have minds and free wills of their own to decide, i.e., stand up against Buck.

But despite my feelings, I was grocery porter and I knew I needed to be walking the grocery in the dark of night, making sure there were no burglars. I tried to see that as a sign that someone saw maturity in me to be able to handle such, but I just felt like someone's slave and that my boss controlled my life.

Once again as I looked around at the dead silence of the grocery in the moonlight, I tried to count my blessings amidst the gloom: I was old enough now, at least, to do what I wanted. I was an adult – a grown man – and thus had the option of going wherever I wanted in life.

Again, people nagged me for doing this instead of college.

"You should be out of here," they would say, suggesting I go teach English in Korea or something, instead of being here.

And indeed – well, essentially – it was criricism by people that caused me to be where I was – as far as not having the confidence to, right after high school, go out in the big wide world and conquer it like a king and - having earlier woken up in the grocery basement alone in the middle of the night – which was so cold the chocolate bars would not melt – made me realize more and more that I was going to have to learn to be alone.

But I could at least feel excited and alone. Excited – cheering to myself like a lone cheerleader cheering without a sports team – thankful that at least I had been entrusted with more responsibility than I had ever had before at the grocery, and that gave me hope. Becoming night porter was one more chance – indeed a big one- to learn the many aspects of running a business, in this case the security of it. Burglars had to be caught, and I was proud that Buck had selected me for it.

And, again, there was a flip side: deep down, I knew it was just someone else that was again using me; I wouldn't have had the job at the grocery if it wasn't for Buck wanting something lucrative, like the witch wanting Dorothy's slippers.

I guessed that Buck must have saved the house from destruction at the last minute so Ann could see it in the worst possible condition without it being completely ruined - indeed he wanted the house - and thus she was mad as Buck deemed necessary at me for it. After all, his goal at the end of all of it was to have our home for extra grocery storage.

And I knew that, again, Buck cared about absolutely nothing else but getting a wedding ring on Ann's finger as soon as I was out of the way.

I stood in the moonlight and looked across the grocery: the aisles where countless weddings had been performed; the deli counter in the back where that unhappy exchange student worked when I was in the eighth grade; the boxes of chocolate that were, again not by coincidence, the favorite brand of Ann's, strewn around the grocery for when Ann might come in to shop at any moment.

The grocery never changed, both in terms of the politics and the layout. Buck never changed his selfish ways as a boss and a person, nor did he ever listen to anyone's suggestions about re-arranging the store for the sake of a little newness; to be updated. Always any suggestions to Buck fell on deaf ears.

And so he – like the town and the look of the grocery itself – never seemed to grow and change; never seemed to go forward. But, again, my wants and needs had certainly changed amidst all the sameness of these surroundings. But any change – especially internally – always meant some degree of pain.

And so, in terms of being glad for what I had, it was, I obsessed again, all either a cup half full or half empty: the boxes of chocolate surrounding me I could see as propaganda or part of the job that I had waited all my life for. But however full my cup was, I was scared of change.

32

Through the night I walked it. I was grocery porter, again meaning security guard for the grocery, if only for a few days. Maybe I would eventually hold a higher position when I returned. Time would tell.

As I walked – or rather, already marched – I pondered the likelihood of a burglar. Fell had always felt so small and safe, not the atmosphere for someone to break in here with a gun. But you never knew, and I knew that Buck knew how expensive that european chocolate was.

Like the Indians said: "all things connect." And food and the grocery and my fate all went together, if not in the strangest way.

But that's how it was: I was like someone's walking recipe, my future put together by someone besides me who - though I didn't want to accept it – didn't care a thing about me.

I tried to go step after step down the aisles with pride. After all, I had been at the grocery three years now – having started in the 11th grade – and for that I was proud. I knew Buck figured I would, again, have quit by now. But I didn't let his verbal abuse get to me and I never would, even when we became related, and when that happened I would have to welcome Buck into the family.

The bulbs above me were dull — everyone in town — and all of Missouri – seemingly asleep except for me. The world again seemed to stand still, as it always felt anyway when I was deep in thought. It was almost as if I was going to see a ghost it was so dark and quiet.

I knew my father would be proud that I was grocery porter and at the same time, I knew Buck wanted to feel that his father would have been proud of him for being grocery manager and owner, even if the only reason for business was, again, all the tourists on the way to that arch thing and the meteor hole.

I had never known my father or Buck's, but I sensed they both must have been quite business-minded, as the grocery was very much their dream too, and my father worked under "Grandfather" Mellon here.

Indeed this grocery had a rich history, long the site, again, of a variety of events throughout the year. And, as always, Buck charged a fee every time which, of course, went right into his pocket instead of toward community charities and organizations. But I couldn't say a word.

I yelled out. HELLOOOOO, wanting to hear an echo because I was lonely. But of course, instead, I heard nothing, feeling maybe being alone was better anyway. It was a nice August night out. I tried not to think of the more exciting places I could be. But then, I'd never known them anyway.

Maybe a man could live on an island alone. Because wasn't that what I was doing, alone in that grocery late at night in that town in that world, with no other planet to go to?

But you could only be alone so long until you just had to have people to help you learn and, too, the joy of being others' teacher: you giving of yourself to help someone else, even though you had yet to help yourself first. And all of it a heaping helping within only so much time to do something for the world, and then you either went into that supposed light or lived again, the light much less scary in my opinion, I not wanting to tread this stressful earth all over again.

And so there I was, as if on an island alone while also a shrinking man, soon to be smaller than a grain of sand, hardly remembered, hardly anything experienced.

And yet I was happy, if only because I knew my surroundings. An environment that both bit at me as to what it had done to me and thrilled me as to what I could do with it. Back and forth I went in unsureness, never knowing what I wanted, an immature wandering porter living an adolescence that may never end — destined, if not for always, to be young at heart, and to look young and hate it.

The speakers on the walls seemed peaceful now. No manipulating music blasting from their wires and plastic — a time of peace for them and I, the chocolate bars seeming on the verge of saluting, with me fantasizing that only I and the aliens saw it. Aliens that may one day communicate telepathically with me and give me a reason why I've been through what I have and what I can help them do.

Maybe someday it would be like that. Maybe the time would come when I would have more excitement than with what comes from my routine. Perhaps something incredibly mysterious would happen to me, and I was selected as almost the only person on earth to communicate with other worlds wearing a grocery apron.

It could happen. A meteor had crashed here already. And so wouldn't aliens want to look for it? And I, being lonely, would be-friend them as much as I had Dale, oh forlorn Dale in the woods, if only for someone to talk to, to pour out my problems to and tell my dreams.

I stood there among the fruit, hoping that, if I re-incarnated, I would be a happy banana. One that would appear in some far, far away planets King Kong-like movie and be a species of plastic fruit that would become a staple in alien beings films, I not affected by a "bad apple" that was a boss that became a stepfather.

33

I laid there in the middle of the night on the mattress, deep in thought. The springs squeaked as if to directly say I was sleeping on a cheap third rate mattress because that was how high my boss and future stepfather regarded me: someone to use; someone to kick around and throw onto a cheap mattress for bedtime. The mattress was uncomfortable and not just because it was third rate, but because it reminded me of prison movies where inmates slept without pillows, the conditions so harsh and uninviting.

Not that prison was supposed to be a glorified motel, but it was just that I was not a criminal; I knew I was a hard working, decent person who had not broken the rules of society and instead deserved to be a vital part of it, not kicked out of my own house for things I did not do. But no one ever said life was fair.

I wished I could have just accepted things like that, and that was it. But by human nature, I wanted more; I wanted much, much better.

I looked out the storeroom window with mixed feelings as to the important things that were coming. I had never in my life been subject to the pain of so much change although, like everyone, I always felt stress when I was going to, say, have new teachers every year. Back in those school days, I had never found a way to maneuver into the "popular set" at school, i.e. the popular people who seemed to push out people like me, even though many of them were my relatives.

Pebbles - upon which sat that park bench and payphone I had seen all my life - led from the exit of the grocery to the front door of my house, the area a small hammock I knew I would miss when I entered soldierhood.

But the sudden change of possibly leaving forever was not the foremost thing on my mind. The whole front yard had been turned into a car part frenzy as, before Buck knocked on the door several hours ago and began his final "trick," I had been trying to get as much of my lifelong hobby done before "time ran out."

Through the basement window, I stared out at our yard across the way in wonderment. The lawn was covered over with auto metal, screws all over the tops of them, rusted pliers that succumbed to the rain.

Beyond the autoed lawn, in what would be a kind of a shrine to my memory, this grocery stood like a place for the needy: for tourists to stop and buy candy and residents with nothing better to do but come in and say hi.

In the middle of everything, I saw the spot where I always swooped down like Superman from my window on the rope, realizing how easy such fantasy of then was and now, with that chapter in my life gone, how real war and manhood were as they both battled between each other in the mirror.

I thought of the town going on without me: someone else would be bagging groceries. The homeless man in the woods might be starving soon at least if, again, he didn't find someone with as big a heart of mine to bring him food and drinks and cigarettes, and there were few other than me who were as lonely and gullible to bring him those things for years just for someone to talk with.

I knew I was a rarity: there was no one as eccentric and no one as kind half the time. The other half of the time I was regretting that I was too nice. Hard on myself I was that I was not more aggressive to keep people from taking advantage of me: for free food; for a ride in my car so they could save gas. I had been used by so many people for so long I had forgotten just how many years it had been going on.

But I did know it had been going on much too long in that town I was finally saying goodbye to. One where I had lived a lifetime.

34

There she was. And because I had hardly recognized myself when I looked in the mirror my perspective of her was different for the first time, knowing she was looking at me with burn marks on my face and arms.

"Hello James" Darlene said, standing with me in my new home – the storeroom – an hour before she punched in that morning, I already done with the grocery except for porter duties.

I knew sometimes she was an early bird to work, but this was special: we were alone together in my "room." I turned on the radio to classical music, we about to dance. For once, I could see something positive coming: my "last dance" in that town.

"I heard what happened, James, and I'm sorry," said Darlene. I was surprised she knew I existed. "See James," she said, "you appear very young. That's why people don't take you seriously. But you will make it because you can't give up."

I was taken aback with flattery.

We embraced, our hands on each others shoulders, then hugging each other and finally dancing. Oh, I will never forget that dance. It is the best thing that ever happened to me. I needed it after all I had gone through. We danced among the boxes of chocolate bars as if in a cemetery, and I had come back from the dead to dance one more time. Darlene showed me how to waltz. It was so much fun. She was my friend.

"Darlene," I said, "Do you want to marry me?"

I received a resounding "no" said kindly as possible, which I expected, the same answer from the same question I had long asked her.

"But we can be friends?" I said.

"Sure, James, sure we are always friends."

And she wasn't calling me "honey"! And we danced. And it was so nice. Not since the prom had I done this. And so I would have had two dates in my life so far. And something to write about in my journal. At least I had gotten something out of the "fire" that was as if I was in hell. At least I got to dance with her before I left. It was happening, indirectly, because of the pressure Buck put on me, this my outlet, my safety valve from it.

And so for once his manipulation – and that subsequent fire – had done me so some good. It was like finding the good in divorce or anything essentially tragic. I knew I would be cut out of the will, but for a few minutes right then I did not care. It was not bothering me. I loved it. How I wanted her. How she – Darlene – again kept me going.

The smell of the chocolate made us both want to rip open the boxes and eat it. But we laughed to each other about it, knowing Buck wouldn't like that. We both valued our jobs, even though surely neither of us was going to have any part of the grocery left to us no matter how hard we worked. But we both knew such was life - it had nothing to do with where we lived - dealt we did with our situations.

Then we sat on the chocolate boxes and just talked. It was such a wonderful conversation. Darlene told me how she had always wanted to be a professor, and how she hated people seeing her for just her looks. She said she didn't have the confidence to try academics. And I told her I had hated school and didn't want to go to college. It was such that neither of us had ever liked school or were college material. We were just rural people, and small things made up happy. I didn't let on to her that I had already found all that out about her from spying on her through her window.

"Buck is very unhappy," said Darlene. "He covers it up by acting macho and picking on you."

"I knooooooow" I said with a long slur.

"Did you know I'm going into the army largely because of his coaxing?" I asked her.

"I figured that, James," she said.

"I know he didn't decorate the grocery every day like it was the Fourth of July and blast patriotic music from the speakers every day for nothing. But he's very business-minded. He's obsessed with that house. And he will give anything to get you out of the way of it."

Of course, such did not surprise me. It did, however, confirm for sure all the suspicions I had about Buck using me over the years. All the times sitting in the yard and putting together the car parts had been an act. Buck had, my mind obsessed once more, just wanted something.

But at least I got that dance. And that conversation with Darlene. It would always be the greatest thing that ever happened to me. It was what I had been hoping and praying for for so long: that she would notice me.

And though my mother now did not claim me, at least I could leave on the army bus Saturday knowing that at least some good things had happened from all of this: I had danced with Darlene; We had talked; She gave a part of herself to me. I had had enough happiness from all that to last a lifetime.

And we danced some more. And it was so nice. It felt like the first time in my life I was truly - even if for a moment - away from my problems. Squeezing Darlene's

Miss America body with her showing me how to waltz, well, I was a guy on cloud nine.

There were things I had lost that week of my life: my mother would never see or trust me the same; I would never trust Buck again. But like a person on their deathbed having their final conversation with friends and loved ones, that was my "last dance" in that town. I needed to savor it. Nothing like it would ever happen again in my life the same. It was as un-doable again as high school: once you graduated, it would never repeat itself.

Somehow I knew this was the only dance I was ever going to have with Darlene. Soon she would punch in for work and it would be back to reality. I had to do neatness inspections. Like Cinderella, the clock was going to strike one. I better enjoy this, I thought.

As the music played, I thought about what I was supposed to be doing: straightening items on the shelves for the day's operation; watching for burglars. Buck came anxiously down the steps, he then standing there impatient.

But for once I didn't care if Buck was mad. For once, I was going to have a little fun. Just this once. This one last dance of mine, of ours, of a man's life.

And we waltzed amidst the chocolate, the boxes of them like an audience watching me learning to slow dance. And for once I didn't mind that this basement was my new home for a few days.

A few more waltzes. It was so nice. My arms on Darlene for the first and perhaps the last time, for who knew if I would live through the war, but if not, because of that dance, I would consider myself more than a statistic as I looked down at the earth from the clouds as a fighter pilot about to be blown up and killed. I would be a person and a man, not a boy. A person with feelings and a real man with character who won the respect and heart of who he wanted. There's something to be said about not giving up, and I never would.

I had tried not to trip and fall as we waltzed. I was such a klutz. But Darlene and I both did pretty well. And when the dance ended she hugged me, even though it was like she pitied me.

"James?," she said.

And I said "What?"

And she said "Don't change."

That was such a nice thing to say.

"Time to get to work, James" said Buck.

And I climbed the stairs for almost the last time for a long time up to the main grocery.

35

The next day I went over to my "former" residence to gather my things. It wasn't good, my mother not even saying hi when I walked in on her; she cooking in the kitchen, and, for the first time, it not to be a meal for me.

"Hello, mother."

"Hi James, how are you today?"

I was excited that she at least spoke to me. But I could tell Buck had a tight grip on her. Thus his plan had gone through, though he hadn't let the house burn as much as I thought.

The kitchen looked so lived in. And it was. So many memories of eating at the wooden, crump laden table that I had come to love, especially now that I essentially didn't have it anymore.

I decided to let my mother be and walked into the living room to go up the stairs. Peanut butter jars — empty mostly — were scattered all over, meaning company was not scheduled to come.

I looked at the phone that never rang. And at our door that was never knocked on. And it did again seem like things would never change. At least if you could say, people didn't. My mother would surely always be eccentric as much as Buck was selfish, and Darlene was — even though she could cover it up with her dazzle — insecure to the bone.

I didn't know then how smart I was. I never gave myself credit for my good qualities, such as just plain trying to be a good person. But being nice had a disadvantage in that people would try to get what they could from you, with the only other alternative not having anyone to talk to — to be with socially — at all.

And so I was now really just a guest in that house. A visitor. A person that did live a lifetime here who was now coming to get their stuff because they were — or already had — moved out. It made me sick to think I couldn't do anything about it because I wanted the job I did, and to come back to it someday, though I knew Jamie would never promote me. Still, I loved the grocery. It — and Darlene — were, I obsessed again, the only things that had ever kept me going.

I started up the steps. They always gave the same creaking sound. That something I would miss — the familiar creaking of that aging house when you put weight on it. I wondered who would live here 100 years from now? Probably someone related to Buck. He had as much control over such as the arch in St. Louis had control over tourism there and here, for without it hardly anyone would ever stop in the grocery, sort of like what if the Leaning Tower of Pisa was straightened? Economic havoc all right. Don't bite the hand that feeds you.

There I was: eighteen-year-old James Michael Woods who wanted to do something like being king of an island but was instead the ousted prince hopeful of the grocery. Yes, it was unfair. Yes, I had known something bad of some kind was coming. I just wished, as I looked back on "the climax", that it was still many years away, instead of massive hurt exploding in my face when my mother and Buck opened that door.

My life began to flash before me, to a time long ago before I had even been in a school, when my life was still innocent, I being tiny and taken care of. But that was many, many yesterdays ago, and I had to put the past behind and carry on.

And I would, leave for the army Saturday, the storeroom instead of my former bedroom having been my final residence.

I stood at it for what might be the last time. My former bedroom, already beginning to fill up with soup cans and chocolate, for Buck had waited so long for it he had started even before I came to gather my things, no matter if it was hurtful.

The rope aged and rotted too. There it still was, tied to my bedpost, a shrine to the memory of my childhood when I would swing on it out the window. Buck would probably throw it away, never realizing the memories it held for me. For like the fact that animals were looked down upon in Russia because they did not work, Buck saw in everyone and everything he came across as either having business potential for him or not.

And I realized he had put the rope back there again - from having temporarily been tied to the bathroom window - to bother me more, to remind me that now the rope - and my room - were no longer mine. People – namely Buck – didn't change, and perhaps neither did life situations. Four walls were going to be four walls. Like a ghost that followed a frightened family to their new home after they fled in terror, the barracks would be four walls on weekend nights as well.

Maybe I should nickname myself Four Walls if that was how it was always going to be for me socially? For, again, I could guess very well that just because I moved, it did not mean I– or my situation – would be any different.

Still, I would meet new people, as I never had during the almost nineteen years this had been my room.

It was ironic: my room so neat, yet peanut butter jars littered the living room. My mother, strangely, picked up after me in my would-otherwise-be-messy room but seemed to have this thing with loving seeing empty peanut jars everywhere. At least she had told me that. Like school yearbooks being my friends as I looked at them on Friday and Saturday nights, so the peanut butter jars kept my mom company when I was not around to do so.

Peanut Butter. Publications. Again and again the two things went through my mind as I watched what was mine all my life – my bedroom – start to change into a place for storage. I would take the yearbooks with me to the army. My mother would continue to gobble down peanut butter. Nothing would change, aside from my mother's name changing from Woods to Mellon as fast as lightning could strike after I left.

Would it be like I had never existed? Wasn't there some way I could leave my mark on the town, on the situation? Was the only way to do so to hang in there to the very end? What else could I do? If only I could come back to haunt Buck one day if he did not do such to me first. And if he did, Buck would be a doozy of an annoying ghost.

So many essential ghosts that would always follow me: even those in the safety and comfort of this last time in my room, if you could still even call it mine. It could perhaps better be said that I was plagued by life's demons, all of them who cringed at my good heart.

It was almost as if I needed an exorcism to calm the emotional storm inside me. I needed a funeral home to be entertained by the theatrical nature of those who worked in it so my life would have a bit of fresh entertainment.

And there was the second-floor bathroom. Burn marks now led to it from the oven up to where the "unforgettable" happened, as Buck had purposely poured a line of gasoline from the downstairs oven with cookies up to where I was. The bathroom would never seem the same either – even when its burn damage was repaired. For it was as if I had died in it, though not actual, physical death. Instead, the attempted death of my hopes, my spirit.

So to me, the bathroom where I loved playing with my boat in the bathtub was now in itself a permanent shrine to my memory that no one would ever understand the way I did.

It was almost as if the whole second floor of the house played funeral music that blended with the patriotic music at the grocery next door. And together, I imagined the two tunes being for me, the tomb of the unknown but only known as "James." Was it like I came back to life and was living on borrowed time, like a ghost: as if I could see everyone, but they couldn't see me, the "real me?"

Never again would anything surrounding me be the same. Only as a guest would I ever come to this house again if even allowed to by my now bitter mother and boss and future stepfather who wasn't nice.

And so would it be too painful to visit? Possibly. But I wanted to see my mother Christmases and all, even if I also had to see who I almost couldn't claim: my future stepfather.

No friends or romances. No siblings. I stood alone that August morning wondering why the feeling of manhood was for me such a long way off.

I had decided I was not going to take the piggy bank with me on Saturday. A symbol of my past it was, as far as I was concerned. Like the taken apart car whose parts went back and forth between my closet and the yard, I had never completed filling the piggy bank to the brim with coins since I had gotten it for my seventh birthday.

You could see chips in the paint from where I had dropped it and glued it back together during Saturdays of so long ago when there was just nothing to do on non-school days.

There were still a few unpopped popcorn kernels that you could hear if you shook the thing, part of an idea I had to copy my mother when I first got the item from my aunt: I was going to try to be the one in Missouri who had a piggy bank with more popcorn kernels in it than anyone else, an idea I hoped would start a state contest similar to my mothers peanut butter eating.

But somehow as even just a week went by, I remembered, the idea turned sour and I forgot about it. Then school starting, life's pace quickening.

I had been so incredibly bored the present summer that I figured things could only get better. Such a thought, I knew, may be too far-fetched considering my mother had disowned me. But to paraphrase an old saying, "I would learn and learn, and with every goodbye I would learn."

By human nature, I did want people to notice me; to be babied, pampered, taken care of. I did not want to believe that no one wanted me around and that no one would miss me when I left in a few days. I wanted to feel that the people of that small enclave where I grew up would feel there was a hole in the town with me not in it. But no, without me on the town would go.

I hated that my mother had returned from the year's contest only to be put in a bad mood as to Buck's plan, for in past years the contest had always been enough fun for her to make up for another year of not having a social life.

I knew my mother had had a good time at the contest. She always did.

I would not know until long after I had left for the army – and been disowned – that she had had me in her will to receive everything she owned from almost the very moment my father had died in war.

I came to find out – as all did in their adult life – that people were very private about things like both incomes and wills, and my mother thus declined to ever discuss either with me.

When I found out I would have otherwise gotten everything, I then truly hated Buck with a passion, just as much as I appreciated him during the times when he had been the only person in town that would talk to me or have anything to do with me besides my mother, the homeless man or Penelope.

I looked around my bedroom. My earliest memories of it seemed like so long ago indeed. Someone else would occupy it someday. But to me, my loneliness and emotions were forever embedded into it. It was as if houses – as if bedrooms like this – did have memories. And just the same, the times of my hopes and victories – such as when I finished high school and came home from graduation only to cry on my pillow wearing my cap and gown – would be part of any bed to ever be in that bedroom that was never again to be mine.

My mother walked by my room carrying a laundry basket. She didn't have anything to do any more than me. Still, I could not be her, and thus I could not know all the responsibilities and problems she had. It just always seemed like I was the only one with problems. Observing my mother, though, maybe such wasn't so.

A few times over the years, my mother hired someone to help clean the house. But they never stayed long, and I could never figure if it was because nobody wanted to do the low end jobs or because our living room was filled with empty peanut butter jars or both. Probably both. But more, I think, because of my mother's obsessive talk about the same things again and again – namely the always coming yearly peanut butter eating contest – and she kind of scared people away. She rather acted the way my eyes bulged with redness and made people wonder about me, be unsure about me and not know how to act in my presence. And so they would rather flee or be mean rather than try to understand me.

One time, I remembered my mother going over the edge with a hired "maid." My mother opened her big mouth and said "There's nothing wrong with the job you do. Everyone has a chance in the United States."

Well, the woman didn't return the next day and my mother, being an airhead, wondered why.

But I knew my mother couldn't help the fact that her mouth got her in trouble. I could have said to my mother, "why did you have to say that?" Indeed saying that to my mother might have helped her realize her faults; But I just let it go.

36

A few minutes before I left the house, I had stood up to leave the kitchen table.

"No, don't leave," my mother said, feeling she was in my face too much and proceeded to leave the kitchen herself.

"I'll leave you in peace. I'll see you tonight, darling. I'm going walking."

"I'm working late tonight. Remember, I'm the porter. And I don't live in this house anymore so you won't see me later tonight."

"Then" she said, not knowing how to finish the sentence and kissed me.

I started to walk out the door to walk across the pebbles that often haunted me since I had seen them for as long as I could remember.

At the same time I was almost out the door, Penelope came toward the house and I dreaded hearing her problems. But we were cousins, and I couldn't turn away family. One of the things I hated about Fell was that everyone was somehow related.

"Hi kid" said Penelope, shaking my hair with her hand, ever a sign that one appeared young, which I could not stand.

I wished I could lock the front door, for she and all my other relatives felt they could just walk right in, which she proudly did.

Penelope sat down on the steps and felt the joy of human contact in her own lonely life. It was good for both of us, even though we didn't have much in common. She remembered being in elementary school with me. We always talked about Mrs. Smith's music class, but I didn't want to look back now.

It wasn't very nice of Penelope, I thought, to wear such heavy perfume. It did not make men any more attracted to her as she was already very chubby. She was so thankful to live in that area – the "Gateway to St. Louis " – and so I saw her as very boring, very easily satisfied. Both of our mothers had always been personal friends with all our teachers.

At that particular moment I wanted to be alone, feeling I couldn't wait to get away from people once I was around them. Perhaps I was happy without people. And Penelope and I were going in different directions. She wanted to be a high school math teacher in Fell the rest of her life. I wanted to never come back, save for the grocery and Darlene.

We always talked about nothing but Penelope and her problems, and I didn't feel like playing pseudo-psychiatrist, at least for the moment.

Since I was 2 I had grown up with this cousin, she born 2 years before I was, and I was finally going to be through with her. We had been through school, and always she had ultimate goals like perfect Sunday School attendance while I often had trouble staying awake in class.

She looked in every way destined to be a secretary or librarian. She wore thick-rimmed glass and might as well be a book editor with a ponytail that took those long lunches. She was chubby; I was thin. I was lazy: She, again, always made straight A's. I felt a twinge of jealousy that, academically, I had not achieved what she had.

I had never been an academic scholar. As to that, my mother never put pressure on me for Ann herself had never continued her education past high school. But she was a mom no matter what and I loved her, despite no college degrees.

Penelope had few friends. And those she did have, like with me, actually used her for her car. They never asked her why she didn't drink, I knew, for then she might drop them and they would have to ask their parents for gas money. People never asked me such questions, either, when they wanted something.

Penelope often went on about all the un-godliness of the world; it so boring to listen to. It was a sad fact that Penelope was boring, but that did not make her a bad person.

I had been with her on church retreats, and she was always the nicest one there, the one that the "adult chaperones" trusted most not to get into mischief.

I was so tired of seeing Penelope's face every other day, as that was how it was in such a small town where you constantly bumped into people you knew. It was, again, almost like being on an island, you sort of stuck, especially when you didn't have the money and resources to move away and even if you did, there was the "emotional" as to facing the fear of the unknown.

Penelope would surely live in Fell all her life. And she would, again, become a teacher in the local school system if only because she was so boring she didn't want anything more. A boring person would be quite happy in Fell.

I wondered if Penelope would ever have a boyfriend. It was sad to think she might never find anyone, might be an old maid but still, you didn't miss what you never had.

And if she did find someone to marry, she would probably ruin it by boring them to death anyway or doing weird things like reading encyclopedias to her impregnated stomach in the hope of having babies born geniuses, like she used to talk about. And I realized this was the last conversation we might ever have together.

37

The military bus pulled up and its doors opened like a shark opening its mighty jaws to eat anyone or anything in its path it could. But I did not mind this beginning-ending. I would be the most experienced one on the bus at all when it came to dealing with war, again having always been at such with myself.

Some on the bus had been among the most popular in high school. But now all were in the one social class of soldierhood.

I looked at all their confident faces. And yet indeed there was no confidence in any of them, only fear of not being accepted for whatever reason, that itself being so adolescent.

And so it had come. The Fell chapter in my life had passed. I would now see the masses used to defend the masses, not just one person used to get one thing, though it was the same idea.

The bus slowly began to gain speed out.

Endings were sad, yes, and there was no telling who on this bus would lose their lives in battle. But it would just mean dying sooner than most people. Death was going to happen to all of us eventually.

What bothered me more was that I did not have to choose this. I could have stayed and worked at the grocery or gone to college. But I always knew I would do what Buck wanted and what Buck had always stressed to my mother: that I would grow up a lot if I were a soldier. I never did argue with Buck, something I regretted. But it was hard to argue with him. He was that kind of person.

The army bus went past the town's buildings. Past the high school then the dusty library. All of it one of a kind to me, for there were too many memories, too many ties with people for it to ever be the same somewhere else in my life again.

There was something everyone on the bus had in common besides being somehow related: cigarettes. They all had it in their pockets, even the guy driving. There would be much less time to enjoy that sort of thing in the military. Much more time spent marching than smoking there would be. But there would be free time – at least one day a week off – to enjoy oneself.

It *did* end up being a time of standstill, waiting to go back to my familiar hometown that was comfortable, a situation I had always been in, even if not necessarily happy.

I looked out a window of the moving bus, realizing that one didn't know just what was coming, and neither too did one know how things were going to go.

The bus stopped, everyone but me getting out to eat at some truck stop like diner. I stayed on the bus to eat my peanut butter and jelly sandwich by myself. I always felt I couldn't wait to get away from people.

Bart stepped up.

I had known Bart Bolles, like many of the soldiers on the bus that day, all my life. Bart had to open his big mouth, as when we were five years old and starting school.

"Is that good?" he said, just trying to find an excuse not to like me.

I didn't say anything.

"What, you don't say hi?" he said gruffly.

There was no way to win with him.

The bus smelled almost like the school one, the seats almost the same green.

But it wasn't school. It was a bus on the way to a military base, and we were all fully grown men; carefree kids no more.

A dead silence rang out, characterizing my social life.

The bus again moved. I observed the driver: a husky, middle-aged white. Why couldn't I be him, the grass seeming greener in his yard?

Sometimes I would get excited I WAS finding myself, but it would elude me. Who was I? Who existed beneath that wishy-washy, unsure, insecure man named James Woods? Being socially adept – or getting anything else I wanted with people – seemed as likely as, again, winning the state lottery.

We crossed the state line. Cheers filled the air, though I didn't contribute to it, afraid of fun being made of my squeaky voice as it had always been.

Yes, it would be a test with an interesting outcome: which of us would get to come home, and which would be the casualties?

But to me, a far greater war was the one I had, again, always been fighting with myself.

"Hi James" said someone, making fun of me.

"Hi" I said, though I should have just not responded.

There were laughs.

I wondered how I looked.

I formed comforting thoughts: my dogs over the years. They liked me no matter what. If only people could be so, but instead they were the most intelligent animals and the meanest ones. The driver saw my zombie look.

"Are you okay?" he said.

"Yeah, why?" I said, frustrated at always being asked that.

I hated people's view of me: never happy with me, I scaring them, wanting to be normal. It seemed, socially, I never could be. Always the one different, left out.

There I stayed: in my place with no one, just used to it.

"Do you drink?" people would also ask me.

"No" I would say.

"What do you do then?" they would say. I would say I liked to read, which was true.

No one ever knew I always I looked at school yearbooks instead of read novels.

I again wanted to run, as far as I could, from everything. It reminded me of walking in line at school with my English class to the library, and we of course had to be obedient then too. It felt strange to be doing it as a grown man instead of a young kid but at least I was getting paid for it, and so it had some meaning, unlike those years in school when I just felt like a guinea pig for the teacher's and principals' paychecks.

We would soon be marching and I knew I was analyzing things more than anyone else. I was a thinker. Unlike the other soldiers, I was giving thought to the universe and whether it was endless or not, while they were thinking about sports or other things I never cared about, including alcohol.

I had long ago decided to accept the challenge of being different. And as to that, I thought I would always be alone.

It helped to see everything as more than just everything; every day as more than just another day. Everything could be a learning experience, even just listening to yourself as you breathe, stopping to smell the roses of life and actual roses which, growing up in the Missouri country, I did a lot of.

I was glad I grew up in a place where you had to stop and think. I realize now I was better off than kids growing up in the fast lane of St. Louis, whom I used to envy because they had things like malls and first run movie theatres that we in Fell did not.

Through the nest of secrets and problems that I – like most people – had, I somehow always seemed to find a light at the end of the tunnel of my great insecurities. I saw such a light only because I held on so steadfast to my hopes and dreams, and from that I learned to tune people out; to not listen to the mean things they said and unfriendly ways they treated me and that took quite a will which, fortunately, I very much had.

38

As I stood in the shower, I had flashbacks: of being picked on, laughed at, but didn't want the other soldiers to know. There was pressure to be macho and fearless like the others. If the other guys at the barracks weren't, in fact, fearless, they could sure mask it, something I had never been able to do and so people, again, always asked me:

"Was I all right?"

A question I again got so tired of. But at least I was away from "that town." And yet I craved the familiar: My job at the grocery that I had waited so long to grow up to work at; My mother; My relatives that made up most of the small community that had been all I had ever known.

I had always been able to carry on with the personal philosophy: "So what if others my age were ahead of me in dating and relationships? What did it matter that I had a young face?" I held my head high anyway, accepting the challenge of being different.

Grown man though I was, it still hadn't been easy leaving for the army just shy of my 19th birthday. I felt I had left high school too soon. Even my mother always said I needed one more year of school; needed to be held back.

I thought of that rope tied to my bed at home, the one I used to use to swing across from my bedroom window to the back of the grocery. I did it until my mother told me I was too old for it. What an influence she had on me. After she said that, I never touched it again.

The barracks showed a history: many a young man had come through here, some insecure, some macho, but perhaps most able to fake their confidence. Again, I had realized something about people: you often could not tell by looking at someone what they were feeling inside.

In the corner, as I stepped out of the shower, was a rack of guns. It made me momentarily feel I was in Alaska, of which I remembered reading college students there had gun racks in their dorms. And, too, I compared it to the gun provided me as a grocery porter. Again, was this really the same situation, just a different locale, the more things changing indeed they staying the same? Different gun, same me?

I would have to be sharp in the military: sharp at marching, sharp at aiming and unfortunately sharp at killing.

Was it right to be trained to kill? Was I, deep down, against what the military did? Indeed, too, was it, again, the reality of a different place but the same situation? Me just as alone here as back home? I had always been by myself and not just because I was an only child.

Would I ever answer my life questions: Was war more what was inside of me than what, who, I fought on the outside? Was how I felt about myself and others more me than where I was?

39

"You're very early."

I tried to ignore the comments of the chef.

"You should be out chasing the girls" said the chef.

I wished he would shut up. So what if I always got to chow hall half an hour early? Fellow troops peered through the glass at me, waiting for the bell announcing dinner. It made me feel like a freak in a circus show.

"Why can't people see things the way I do?," I wondered, "Then the world would be so great."

Why, I wondered, did the chef and the other soldiers always look so confident when they really were scared to death inside like me? Why did I have to stand out in the crowd? They did not realize that I had been trained to get to places early. My former boss at the grocery back home, Buck Mellon, would penalize me if I were even a minute late and that had stayed with me into the military and probably for the rest of my life. Then the chef opened his mouth again:

"James, you're 18, but you aren't like everybody else. Look around the cafeteria. No one is here."

Dead silence then rang out loudly through the chow hall, I not knowing just what to say.

"Do you always HAVE to do what everyone else does?" I said.

But it was no use. The chef still did not understand me.

The bell rang and dozens of soldiers came in and lined up behind me. I didn't feel almost 19.

"You're like a little kid" someone said loudly in my ear while standing behind me and then laughed.

I wondered why people made fun of me. Why always me? I felt as if I were a clown jumping from table to table in the chow hall. I was like a different breed, like a strange color contrasting against the other soldiers. But surely their mothers did everything for them too? Surely their parents wrote a letter to the high school protesting the teaching of sex education?

There was only one way to find me: by learning from other people. But I had never been around very great people to be learning from; They were - either in that small hometown of mine or here in the rigid discipline of the military – in a sense using thought control: small towns in the way of gossip; the military in the way of total domination and fear. What was scary was how the two could be related. Gossip – like control – could spread through a small area like fire and dominate people's beliefs so quickly.

I saw what everyone was eating: pizza. It reminded me of Fridays in the school system: Fridays meant pizza with that delicious corn. It was the same here: the best meal was reserved for the last weekday.

I remembered my high school facing the prospect of having a fence and then the ugliness of it getting one. Still, I was "outta there." It was good to be out of school. What confused me – as I looked around at all the soldiers enjoying their dinner – was that there were people here who could hardly – if at all – read or count. Why was it they were not given a hard time about it? I knew I was way ahead of them in one way: my insight into life. They just gave looks of confidence so it wouldn't look good to give them a hard time.

Again life questions: Would I find the true definitions of love and war and in that, find myself? And would I not find those answers on the battlefield but rather deep down somewhere in myself?

A long line was still forming at the chow hall, stretching for what almost seemed a mile, even though the mealtime was almost half over. But I wasn't hungry. I was too depressed to eat, too much on my mind, while all the other soldiers seemed pig-headed, just caring about picking up girls when the only day we had off – Sunday – came around.

Back home that day for me would be church and Sunday School, but here – though there was a chaplain and a Sunday Service – most of the soldiers seemed to have other things on their mind than religion.

I set personal goals for my time here. If I could make just one friend – and help at least one person here with their problems – I would have given a part of myself and would truly have grown.

Because those were the ways I needed to grow: branching out from thoughts of just myself and what is wrong with my life. I had to think about other people and their problems, too.

I knew the hard part hadn't started yet: I had just arrived, and the beginning of something was always the best time. But I did so hope it was happy and fulfilling despite the politics and bureaucracy of any large organization and the sometimes "takes more than it gives" way that was the military.

At least, again, I got something for it, unlike high school where, again, I worked for society for no pay, even though I got academic credit for the time. Here, despite the stresses, there would be returns, finally, from society. I could soon, among other things, feel good that I did something for my country. At least if I got to live.

I knew what my mother would say: she would say I could run rings around the other soldiers as far as succeeding. But that was my mother, and not everyone in the world I dealt with was going to be like her. Very much so we were now apart from each other anyway and not, I knew, just because of physical distance but also - more - because of a long planned out barbeque by one Buck Mellon, who by now was almost my stepfather. But if Buck was now almost a relative – even if just by marriage – I couldn't change it ever, ever, ever anyway.

I couldn't believe the day had come and I had arrived. While I saw the military coming in my life for as far back as I could remember, I certainly did not think my childhood would end so quickly. And the real world made me want to, again, run home to my mother, I partly wishing I could live in that house with her for the rest of my life and sneak food to the homeless man until his dying day.

But I couldn't do that. The right thing was to move on. And indeed, it was long overdue for me to leave that little enclave and branch out to other things. I felt that to be the adult I wanted to and should fully become, I would have to form the difficult habit of not looking back.

I laid on my bed in the barracks thinking of the generations to come that would grow up in the same town that I did – indeed I would be somehow related to almost everyone that grows up there in the years to come – and what I would always have in common with all the towns future generations would be resources: I had the resource of a family name that kept me from getting beat up at school; most anyone that grows up there would have the benefit of connections – of getting things because they know people – class office, such as president, in high school, and the scant few jobs in Fell along with the many in St. Louis that indeed required fitting in enough to know someone who likes you, and you get hired that way.

Oh I only cared – and still did as to that town - about working at the grocery. Even now, a lifetime later - from age 5 to now almost 19 - it was the only place in this world – in fact – that I cared about working at the rest of my life, even though that may seem a bit sad as far as goal setting, but I had waited and worked too long to let go of my dream of owning and managing the grocery. And there were too many memories associated with it and the adjacent house where I grew up to permanently – in my life – leave it. Again and again that went through my mind, even there at the barracks a world away.

The human element was interesting to watch, and indeed the whole world changed when you switched from talker to listener. If the eyes tell all about a person, don't also one's own ears tell one all about people around one at all too?

"Did you know that Danny's weirdo mom came to the barracks and tried to take him away because she was worried about him, and legally he could not go and they asked her to leave the property?" I heard a soldier say to another soldier.

And Danny WAS like me: lots of problems; a mama's boy. He – unlike everyone I saw – looked like he didn't have it all together, rather the mirror image of myself I always wondered existed. I listened further to the two soldiers gossiping:

"And I wonder if he will make it as a soldier. There are many here, I see, who do not seem ready for the military, albeit for life after high school at all."

That described how I rather felt, even a year and two months after graduating. And so I was not alone in my real-world fears: others felt it too. But you would never know it by looking at them. Absolutely everyone but Danny and I looked so confident, and I didn't know why. Why did he and I seem to be the only insecure ones who stood out in the crowd as to it, while everyone else seemed able to blend into the woodwork, not sticking out at all?

Later I heard:

"Danny ended up leaving with an honorable discharge. He probably can't stay with anything or do anything right in the first place, he's so nervous." And the two soldiers laughed.

It took branching out from a lifetime in that town to come across someone like me.

I thought about what Danny must be going through. Maybe he grew up in a small town like me, and never really had anyone. There was no telling.

But I could guess that Danny had probably been through many of the things I had, such as never having a social life. I could guess that Danny might be back home in his room, peering out the window for hours like I used to, deep in thought.

And his mother probably cooked everything for him and bought all his clothes, and probably would for much of Danny's adult life, at least for a while, as long as his mother was able to.

And so Danny, like me, wasn't used to life after high school yet either. And so why didn't people show compassion for insecure, young-looking people like Danny and I, instead of trying to find an excuse not to like us all the time? Things didn't always work out; pan out right. I knew that all too well. I'd had many disappointments with people, largely people who had always known me not being willing to give me another chance even though I had improved.

I hoped for Danny that he was not going back to the situation of everyone knowing he came back as he returned to the town he was from. But deep down, I knew he was, and the same thing could happen to me if I didn't work at it. My people there, as I called them, would always hold it against me that I had failed the military.

But would they really have room to talk anyway, they never having even tried beyond that town?

And again and again I pushed myself, feeling unable to win, to be satisfied.